PRAISE FOR

KISS THE SCARS
ON THE BACK OF MY NECK

"Joe Okonkwo has a keen eye and ear for the way human beings talk to each other and think about themselves. The stories in *Kiss the Scars on the Back of My Neck* range from the woundedness of the modern age to the defiant power of the glorious Harlem Renaissance, shimmering from start to finish with passion, love, rage, loneliness, and danger. A remarkable examination of the human condition."

—William J. Mann, author of
Hello, Gorgeous: Becoming Barbra Streisand

"Joe Okonkwo presents a world of hurt—the walking wounded dragging themselves through the wreckage they themselves sometimes created. His voice, a steady hand on the back of your neck, forces you to look at his deeply flawed characters. You can dislike them, you can judge them, but you cannot turn away, so compelling is his examination of his characters' emotional truths. To read this collection of stories is like taking a master class in writing literary fiction."

—Lambda Literary Award Finalist Larry Benjamin, author of
The Sun, The Earth & The Moon and *In His Eyes*

"Vivid, taut, slyly funny, bitchy, steamy, kinky, painful, melancholy, tender—all those words and more describe the stories contained here. Okonkwo fluidly moves between eras, points of view, and narrative voices to spin a collection of tales that capture people—Black and white, gay, straight and ambiguous, bougie and low-down—at their best and worst, striving for sex, status, and true love. Whether the conflicts are mothers and sons, bisexual love triangles or schoolmates turned lovers, the characters in Okonkwo's stories pinball against one another in surprising ways, many of them reuniting once more in the final title story, a moving and complex crescendo."

—Tim Murphy, author of *Christodora and Correspondents*

"Joe Okonkwo's storytelling talents are on full display in his new collection. Moving through a range of eras and settings, the finely drawn characters in these nine short stories navigate sex, love, power, betrayal, and belonging as they strive to live as their full and veracious selves."

—Lisa Ko, author of *The Leavers*

"Joe Okonkwo does deep character work. Centering Black voices, queer voices, and femme voices, *Kiss the Scars on the Back of My Neck* presents unforgettable characters in stories that are equal parts heartbreaking and hilarious, and, at times, achingly sexy. In this far-ranging collection—moving from Prohibition-era jazz clubs to the Reagan '80s to present-day hook-up app culture, swinging from child narrators to single mothers, and including several thrillingly-linked stories—Okonkwo explores what it means to be human in all its glorious messiness. His characters throb with desire, fumbling to love and feel loved in the only ways they know-how. In Okonkwo's stories, there are no easy answers, no black-and-white, only, as one of his characters notes, 'oases of gray.' Musical references abound. Makes sense, as one of the great pleasures of reading Okonkwo's work is the sounds of his sentences, the poetry of his language. I finished this book feeling richer, wiser, and more grateful to be alive."

—Rahul Mehta, Lambda Literary Award-winning author of *No Other World* and *Quarantine*

KISS
THE SCARS
ON THE
BACK
OF MY NECK

STORIES

JOE OKONKWO

AMBLE
PRESS
Ann Arbor
2021

Amble Press

Print ISBN: 978-1-61294-203-2

Amble Press First Edition: August 2021

Several of the stories in this collection have been published
previously in slightly different formats.

"Cleo," published in *LGBTsr.org*, 2016
"Skin," published in *Chelsea Station*, 2016
"Picnic Street," published in *The New Engagement*, 2018
"The Girls' Table," published in the anthology *Strength*, 2018
"Gift Shop," published in *The Piltdown Review*, 2019
"Fluff," published in *Global City Review*, 2020
"Paulie," published in *Newtown Literary*, 2020

To RJL

"If you are silent about your pain, they'll kill you and say you enjoyed it."

—Zora Neale Hurston

CONTENTS

PICNIC STREET

The home pregnancy test confirmed Justine's worst suspicion. She sat on the edge of the tub in her sister's guest bathroom in her slip and bra. Sweat slicked off her forehead, down her back, and dribbled from her underarms. She barely noticed. She lifted her hand from the tub's rim, intending to rest it on her stomach. But a sob erupted in her chest and flowered into her throat, forcing that hand to change direction. It ended up gnashed against her mouth as she suppressed, if not the sobs, at least the sounds of them. Sounds an eavesdropper might find too raw, too reckless, dangerous.

Her sobbing eased. She doused her face with cold water to prevent puffy eyes and for some relief from the summer heat. She looked in the mirror, realized she'd failed on both counts: Her eyes were bulbous and she was sweating puddles. She dried off and started on her makeup. A woman recently separated from her husband would be gossiped about in this town if she wore makeup on a Saturday—a Saturday morning at that—but she did it anyway. She didn't bother with foundation—in this heat she would sweat it off in two minutes flat—but she did apply eye shadow and took her artful time with her lips. She outlined them and colored them in with feverish red. By the time she finished, her mouth stood out like a flare.

She slipped on her white skirt and yellow chiffon halter top, then glided into a pair of open-back high heels with silk daffodils affixed to the bands. She looked in the mirror again. Except for the bulbous eyes, Justine loved what she saw: a beautiful, thirty-three-year-old Black woman, slim but with enough curves to earn suspicious looks from women in the aisles at Jitney Jungle; whose shapely legs and dainty tits triggered whistles and *hot damns* from men on the street. The other day at the record store a very handsome white man had winked and puckered his lips. She was supposed to be offended that men objectified her. But she liked it. It meant they wanted her, and that meant she still had it. Justine had thought a few times about that white man. Her husband Desmond had decided he didn't want her. Desmond had decided he couldn't and wouldn't touch her.

A sob flowered in her throat again, but she willed it away. She lifted her hand and this time it did arrive at her stomach. It laid there softly before snarling into a fist. Justine thought, *what now?* She'd been asking herself that since she left Desmond last month and returned to her hometown of Winslow, a semi-backwards town of twenty-five thousand in the fully-backwards state of Mississippi. A town where, by 1979, Blacks and whites shared lunch counters, water fountains, and schools, but rarely neighborhoods. Winslow piddled on the coast of the Mississippi River, a mere fifteen minutes from Louisiana if you took the Stonewall Jackson Confederate Memorial Bridge.

Justine went to find her son. Michael Jackson's "Don't Stop Till You Get Enough" kicked out of her sister Loretta's stereo and echoed throughout the house. That song had invaded every stereo and car radio in Winslow. Justine couldn't escape it. She'd been moving swiftly, her heels clickity-clicking over the hard floors. But as she neared Loretta's room, she stepped lightly. Loretta despised noise, especially on Saturday. Growing up she'd always been sensitive to it.

"Paulie? Paulie, where are you?"

Justine heard a little-boy voice coming from the living room:

"What do you think works better—the green piece or the blue piece? *The blue piece. It's prettier.* I think you're right. *Of course, I'm right, Paulie. I know what looks good.* No, you don't. Not always. When we were building the fort, you thought the yellow pieces worked, but they looked dumb. Whoever heard of a fort made of yellow? *Nobody's right all the time. But I'm right* this *time—you said so.*"

Paulie. Talking to himself. As always. Not in the innocuous way most children did when they voiced the actions of a doll, or pretended to be an astronaut piloting a spaceship. Her son conducted full-blown conversations with an imaginary friend named Boris. Paulie talked and answered himself—out loud— as Boris. He'd done it since he was three. She'd wanted to put a stop to it, but wasn't about to deprive him of the one playmate with whom he felt at ease. He never talked to Boris in public. She was grateful for that.

He could have a flesh-and-blood playmate. If I had this baby.

Justine found him on the floor playing with his Legos. Every piece of his deluxe set lay scattered across the floor in front of Loretta's favorite chair. Paulie had strewn his sketch pad, colored pencils, and markers across the chair itself. Justine quickly began to scoop up Legos.

"Baby, your Aunt Loretta's going to have a fit if she sees your toys all over the place."

"But Aunt Loretta stays in her room on Saturdays, Mama."

"That may be." Justine peered over her shoulder for Loretta. "But you never know. She might surprise us."

"Mama? Why do Aunt Loretta—"

"Why *does* Aunt Loretta."

Justine shot him a practiced frown. He picked up bad grammar from watching cartoons. She wanted to ban Popeye and Bugs Bunny—was itching to—but that risked an outcry that would be more trouble than it was worth.

"Why *does* Aunt Loretta stay in her room all day every Saturday?"

"She works hard all week. Sundays she has her church

3

activities. Saturday is the one day she gets time to herself." She frowned again, but softer. "And we have to be considerate. Which means being quiet and not leaving our stuff everywhere. OK?"

She went back to her cleanup.

"Mama? Why doesn't Aunt Loretta like me?"

Justine stopped collecting the Legos, struck, not by Paulie's question, but the soberness with which he'd asked it. Justine wished she could tell him he was wrong.

"Baby," she said, "your aunt doesn't have children of her own. She's not used to having them around."

"But she teaches school."

"Yes…But…she's not used to children in her house. That's different."

"How's it different?"

She was irritated now. He was making this difficult, challenging her when she needed him to simply accept her explanations. "Baby, it just is."

She had almost all the Legos picked up.

"Mama, if Aunt Loretta don't like kids—"

"If Aunt Loretta *doesn't* like kids! And I didn't say that, Paulie."

"If Aunt Loretta *doesn't* like kids, why's she letting us stay here?"

He was sitting with his knees tucked under him, his sweet brown eyes pulsing innocence. She looked right into them and didn't blink. *Because I begged her. Because I got on the phone and told her I had to leave your father and had no other place to go. We were broke. Your father had put us in debt. We were drowning in it. And he wouldn't touch me anymore. I cried and I cursed and I told her she owed me for the way she treated me when we were growing up. Made her feel so guilty, she gave in and even sent me the money for the airfare.*

"Because she loves her family, Paulie. That's why."

All the Legos were back in the box. As she retrieved the sketch pad, pencils, and markers from the easy chair, she saw the cap was off the green marker. It had left a tiny green dot on the dark beige fabric. She railed before she could stop herself.

"Desmond Paul Crane, Jr.! I've told you to be careful with these markers!" Justine yelled as she raced to the kitchen. "You're too careless with your things." She grabbed a cloth towel and wet it. "When you're careless with *your* things, that can affect *other people's* things." She ran back to the living room. "Now there's a stain on your Aunt Loretta's chair—because you were too lazy and too inconsiderate to put a cap back on a marker."

She dabbed at the stain, terrified the dot would bloat into a smudge. Several dabs later, she could still detect a pinprick of green. Tiny enough that Loretta would probably never notice. *Probably.*

Paulie had turned his head aside. He always did that when she yelled. Never cried, pouted, or talked back. He would simply turn away in an elegant gesture of reproach. He'd disappear, abandon her. Justine would have preferred he roll his eyes or curse her out. Then she wouldn't need to regret her temper. More important, she'd know her young son's body was occupied by a nine-year-old child and not the old soul she feared actually resided there. She hated when he disappeared. Hated worse that eerie moment when he returned—that moment like right now—when his eyes linked with hers and seemed to say, *How could you? Was it worth it?*

She kissed an apology onto his forehead. "Let's play someplace else."

"The front porch?"

He'd come back to her. He always did, but she was relieved nonetheless. She exhaled. She hadn't realized she'd been holding her breath.

As they walked through the house, Justine smelled cigarette smoke bleeding from underneath Loretta's bedroom door. She knew her early-bird sister had risen at six and lit up a minute later, that she'd stay in her bedroom all day, smoking and drinking Coke and flipping through *Essence* and *Ebony* and listening to cassettes. She'd dispensed with Michael Jackson and moved on to "Got to Be Real" by someone named Cheryl Lynn. Disco.

Justine loathed it.

Once on the porch, Paulie scattered his Legos and played. Justine parked in a wicker chair and fanned herself with a newspaper. Fanning seemed to escalate the heat so she scanned the front page instead. The lead article speculated that Kennedy would challenge Carter in the Democratic primary next year. A Gallup poll put the Massachusetts senator ahead—58 percent. Carter's critics thought this energy crisis business could topple him. *Good riddance*, Justine thought. His speech on TV last month—about the country's "crisis of confidence" and Americans' unsatisfied longing for meaning—had enraged her. His presumption offended her. She had supported him in '76, but now prayed Ronald Reagan would run. Her Republican epiphany had delighted her many white friends, bewildered her few Black friends, and infuriated Desmond. Her announcement that she was switching parties incited an argument so savage, even now Justine was shocked it hadn't come to blows. Afterward, Desmond said not a word to her—not one—for two heavy weeks. Not good morning, nor good night, nor pass the peas, please.

She turned to watch Paulie, grateful that her nine-year-old was a master at entertaining himself. As an only child, he'd had to be, especially since his skill at making friends fell far short of his prowess for self-amusement. He concentrated on his Lego construction like an engineer, arranging the pieces exactly so, fine-tuning his work while coordinating with Boris.

"Boris, does this look OK? *Looks great to me, Paulie.* Thank you. *You're welcome. Maybe put some more pieces on top. Not those. The red ones.* We're out of red. *OK, the white ones. You always use red too much.* It's my favorite color. *Last week your favorite color was yellow. The week before that it was blue.* Those are my Lego favorite colors. My real favorite colors are turquoise and salmon. *Why can't you have normal real favorite colors?* I guess I'm not a normal kid. Does that bother you? *Nope. I'm not a normal kid either.* I guess that's why we get along so well. *Must be. But sometimes you annoy me when—*"

"What are you guys—I mean—what are you making, baby?" Justine said.

"It's the Empire State Building."

Indeed. Justine made out the tall main stem, narrowing up to the crown-like top. Paulie had even recreated the spire on the building's peak. If he was particularly proud of a creation, he would sketch it with his colored pencils and present it to Justine to hang somewhere. She prized his creativity. It made up for the times he abandoned her.

"Do it—*does* it look all right, Mama?"

"It's perfect."

"We're gonna go there, right? When we move to New York?"

"Yes, Paulie. We'll go there."

"And the Statue of Liberty? And the Natural History Museum for the dinosaurs? And we'll live in Times Square and swim on Coney Island and hopscotch across the Brooklyn Bridge and dance on the West Side like the Jets and the Sharks. We'll do all that when we move to New York. Won't we, Mama?"

"Yes, Paulie. We'll do all of that."

Creative Paulie. He'd taken her plan and made it his own. Brightened it into an innocent version of the escape plan she'd concocted: Get out of Michigan. Come home to Winslow for a year—*and only a year, damn it.* Make Loretta get her a job teaching summer school. Live with Loretta to save money. Move to New York. Divorce Desmond. Maybe remarry. Maybe not. Maybe another Black man. Maybe not.

But now? Her hand drifted to her stomach.

She wasn't sure she could suppress the flowering in her throat this time. She couldn't let Paulie see her cry. Justine fled the porch, past Loretta's four-door Buick Electra hunching in the driveway. By the time she got outside the gate, the flower had closed. She'd made it close. She would not cry. She would not allow herself that purging pleasure. A couple of tears trickled out, but she'd beaten back a surge and she was proud of that. Her head hurt. A guiltless thought pulsed against the ache: *There are clinics in Jackson. I could take Loretta's car. Get it done. Be back in time to pick Paulie up from his swimming lesson at the Y.*

"Don't Stop Till You Get Enough" wailed from a passing car's radio. To counter it, Justine hummed. Something vague that soon veered into a melody from *Les Pêcheurs des Perles*—her favorite opera. She had left her recording of it in Michigan. She'd made that trip to the record store last week to find a new one. Justine laughed. Had she really thought she'd find a full-length opera recording at a rinky-dink record store in Winslow? The closest thing they had was a *Fun with Classical Music* cassette. But she got winked at by that handsome white man, and that had made the trip worth it.

She took in her sister's ambitious house. A handsome, white, two-story house in the second-to-last lot on the south side of Picnic Street. It stood out among the shacks occupied by food stamp and welfare families. Envious Blacks who knew Justine had lived up north and clucked about her humble return to Winslow.

"What you hummin', Justine? Don't sound like nothin' popular. You always did have a thing for weird music that nobody in they right mind would bother with."

Justine didn't need to turn around to know an old and lively nemesis had snuck up on her.

"It *is* popular," she said. "A popular opera."

A lie. *Les Pêcheurs des Perles* was one of the most sublime yet least performed operas in the repertory. Justine turned around. Marla St. Brian stood in front of her, accompanied by her three kids.

Marla snorted. "Yep. Like I said: weird shit can't nobody be bothered with. Nobody 'cept white folks. And you."

Marla's daughter clutched a handful of her mother's grimy beige skirt. Justine guessed she was seven. Marla's older child, a boy about Paulie's age, stood a little apart. A skinny baby bundled in only a cloth diaper drooled in Marla's arms. Justine was dumbstruck. Paulie may have been an old soul, but Marla St. Brian's kids *looked* old. Age licked at their ashen skin. It hollowed their postures to a slump. But it was their eyes that made

8

Justine want to turn away. Weary, placid, brooding eyes. The eyes of the hopeless. These kids would not escape Winslow as she had, would not attain anything better than what they had now. They seemed, somehow, to know that.

"Marla, don't be concerned with what I'm humming," Justine said. She gestured at the three kids. "You have other things you need to be a lot more concerned about, I think."

"I don't give a shit what you think!"

Thin-skinned, Justine thought. *Always was.* She smiled in celebration of the point she'd just scored and in tribute to the old rivalry. Justine and Marla detested each other on sight, Day One of kindergarten. Each girl had had her supporters and detractors, those she claimed as followers and those who scorned her. Befriending one meant earning the other's evergreen disdain. To goad Justine, Loretta had befriended her rival. She'd chit-chat loudly with Marla on the phone, making it impossible for Justine to evade the acid of her older sister's betrayal.

"Ain't seen you since you been back," Marla said. "Guess you too good to associate with the folks you grew up with."

"Marla, since when do you want to associate with me? You never did in school."

"That's 'cause you was a stuck-up bitch."

Marla's son hadn't been minding them, his eyes wandering here and wandering there, fidgeting his weight from one foot to the other. But *bitch* pricked his attention. He stopped fidgeting. His focus zoomed onto the adults skirmishing in front of the nicest house on Picnic Street.

"Don't wanna associate with you," Marla said. "But I wanna hear about your fancy life up north." Marla shifted the baby to the opposite hip. "Must not have been too good if you're back in Winslow. What happened, Justine? Couldn't cut it? Well. That's what happens when Black folks try to act above their station."

This was the most fun Justine had had since she'd come back home. She tittered at Marla's taunts. More than that, she reveled in the envy that bred them. Justine had got out of Mississippi. All Marla ever got was pregnant. Three kids by three different fathers, if the rumors panned out. Justine looked at Marla's stomach. Loretta had been gossiping over the past week, launching speculation about illegitimate baby number four. Marla lived on welfare in a shack across the street. Kept hens in her backyard for eggs and chicken dinners. Loretta said Marla ate so many eggs and so much chicken, they sickened her. Justine scrutinized her favorite enemy, her prematurely thinning hair, and almost felt pity. Almost.

"And how about that fancy husband?" Marla said. "Can't wait to hear *aaallll* about him."

Marla's fat smile startled Justine. It made her nervous. It was the smile of someone who knew something she shouldn't— and relished it. It knocked Justine off balance, but she recovered quickly, like when they had wrangled back in their school days.

"You want to hear about my life up north?" Justine said. "I'll have you over some time. In the name of renewing glorious old friendships."

"We can have tea and crumpets or whatever you and white folks be eatin' up there."

"You can bring dessert," Justine said. "On second thought, bring chicken salad. Be sure to put lots of eggs in it."

Marla thrust the baby back to the original hip. "Justine, you always was an uppity nigger."

Marla's skirt-clutching daughter looked listless from the heat. Her eyes kept fluttering down and popping open again. But her brother's eyes danced from his mother to Justine. He had been standing apart from the two women, but now nudged closer.

Justine shook her head, like a parent exasperated and amused by a ridiculous child. If Marla thought she'd scored a direct hit by blasting out the "uppity nigger" slur, she'd wasted her firepower. Justine Regina-Lee Ward Crane had long ago fortified her defenses against that attack. But she hadn't always been strong. "The Slur" used to wound her. She and Desmond had been shocked when Blacks accused them of assimilation, as if it was dirty. They defied "The Slur" and those who hurled it. They drove big cars, purchased the latest electronics, added needlessly on to their house—and every Christmas morning Paulie bounded out of bed and raced to the living room to be dazzled by a treasure trove of expensive toys. They did well. Until defiance proved costly and debt blindsided them. And was it a coincidence that they started talking about bankruptcy at the same time Desmond stopped making love to her?

"Sticks and stones," Justine sing-songed. She was tired of this game. She needed to check on Paulie and get out of the sun, make calls, find the address of a clinic in Jackson. "I've got things to do." She turned to go.

"Your husband's stick sho ain't no stone," Marla said. "Least not from what I hear."

Justine almost fell down. *Marla can't know*, she thought. *Please god. She cannot know.* She turned around, took in Marla's wide-legged stance, her eyes seething cold triumph.

"That nigger won't touch you no more," Marla said. "What's his name? Desmond? *Please, Desmond. We young. This ain't right. Desmond, make love to me. It used to be so good. Please, oh, please, please, Desmond. Let's get marriage counseling. I can't go on like this no more.*"

Marla's son was riveted. The sleepy daughter was now awake and tuned in. Even the baby perked up.

"Your husband won't fuck you," Marla said, "so you found white men to do it for you."

Loretta.

That. Bitch.

For the second time in as many minutes, Justine almost fell. That thing flowered in her throat. Her sister was the only person she'd confided in about Desmond. Marla had repeated, nearly word for word, what Justine had told Loretta. If Marla knew, Picnic Street knew. If Picnic Street knew, so did Winslow. At least the Black side.

She needed to hold Paulie. The need ambushed her. What a shame that a nine-year-old child who talked to himself was the only person in the world she trusted.

11

She hurried toward the house.

"Lemme know when I'm comin' over for tea and crumpets, bitch!" Marla said.

Justine froze when she reentered the yard. Paulie wasn't playing with his Legos. He sat on the porch, legs crossed, head down. Talking to Boris.

"Boris? *Yeah?* I miss Daddy. *I know.* I'm sad. *Come here.*"

Paulie wrapped his arms around his chest, hugged himself. Rocked and babied himself. Justine shook her head at the irony: an old soul babying himself. And she raged, silently, at Boris. He possessed what she wanted and deserved: Paulie's intimacy, Paulie's attention, Paulie. What a shame, taking a back seat to an imaginary child. Paulie and Boris had each other. Marla St. Brian had her raggedy kids. Who did Justine have?

That flower split her throat again. This time she surrendered to it. Let it blossom. Allowed the petals to unfurl, the leaves to splay out. Paulie had abandoned her again. They all had.

Have they? All?

As Boris consoled her son, her hand, for the third time that still-young day, drifted to her stomach. It laid there. It laid there a long time.

SKIN

I hate my body.

My biceps are puny as plums. My chest doesn't fill out even the smallest T-shirt. My calves are sapling-thin, bone wrapped in flesh. I'm Black, so my ass is supposed to be a buoyant, high-shelf force of nature. In my twenties and thirties it was, kind of. But in my mid-forties the shelf has descended a few pegs and it's ringed with stretch marks. I avoid mirrors. I hurry past windows so I'm not assaulted by my reflection. Selfies are an absolute no-no.

Self-help books tell you to love yourself, to love your body, or at least accept it. They warn about the perils of comparing yourself to others. But it's hard not to, especially right now, because on my computer screen, opened up in Photoshop, is a picture of a guy lying on a beach. His dark curly hair and beard flow, almost seamlessly, into the jungle of hair that carpets his titanic pecs. The flat stomach is hacked up into six distinct sectors. One arm rests behind his head, exposing the vulnerable flesh of his underarm. His other hand teases the waistband of his snakeskin bikini as if he is aching to remove it. His eyes are half closed, his unsmiling mouth half open. It seems to whisper, *Of course you want to fuck me. But you're not worthy.*

I'm a web coordinator at Tapestry, a website for gay men. Our editorial mission is to produce engaging, carefully curated content that empowers our audience to make savvy choices in the realms of lifestyle, fashion, travel, and entertainment, choices that will enhance the user's style and self-assurance so that he can confidently and productively represent the gay community.

But regardless of the altruistic editorial mission, Tapestry is ultimately about one thing and one thing only: hot shirtless men.

That's why this guy is on my screen. I have to prep the image so it can be uploaded to our site. This pic went up today on another gay site and the editors want it on ours to boost traffic. His name is Valero Martinelli-Verdi, but since becoming a breakout star on the reality series *Bluegrass State*, he's shortened it to simply *Valero*. The show is shot in Lemon Pepper, Kentucky, population 6,500. It documents the antics of a cadre of twenty-somethings whose sole purpose is to scandalize the town's residents. Brawling in the streets. Arrests. Interracial couplings. Valero exploded onto the radar of popular culture a year ago, during the 2012 season, when he sauntered down Lemon Pepper's main drag in a neon-orange thong and $350 Gucci flip-flops. During a recent interview, he made a tepid comment supporting marriage equality: *Sure, whatever, it don't bother me. I think I got a gay cousin.* The gay media lit up. "VALERO SUPPORTS MARRIAGE EQUALITY," "REALITY STAR COMES OUT IN SUP-PORT OF SAME-SEX MARRIAGE," and "TV'S HOT-TEST HUNK SUPPORTS US!" were a few of the headlines lasered onto the home pages of gay sites across the web. Valero: the gay world's newest icon.

What if he didn't have that body?

"Terrence, is the Valero pic ready?"

The voice of Chad, our online editor. It leaps at me over the cubicle wall while he sits in his office. I know he hasn't bothered to stand or look up from his computer.

"Almost," I answer.

Moments later I hear Chad conversing with the fashion

editor, Brandon. Seems like gay white guys in their twenties and thirties are all named Chad or Brandon or Darren or Evan.

"Like, I got a resume today," Brandon says, "for the junior editor position? The guy's cover letter says he has thirty years' experience. He presents it like it's an asset. He's gotta be in his fifties. Maybe even sixty." I can't see them over the cubicle wall, but I imagine Brandon—from the perch of his young, blue-eyed, peroxide-blond supremacy—just shuddered. "What should I do?"

I hear paper tearing. Chad must have snatched the offending resume and ripped it to pieces. "He wouldn't fit in here. He wouldn't *get* us."

He says this with a pretense of sympathy, as if rejecting the fifty-year-old is for the man's own pitiful sake. I have a moment of fright: I'm not that far from fifty.

Chad suddenly materializes at my cubicle. "Is the Valero pic ready?"

Tattoos engulf his arms and hands. They creep up both sides of his neck like climbing vines, overrunning his olive-complected skin. I know from the superabundance of selfies plastered on social media that his entire body is engraved with tattoos. *What a shame*, I think. Because, except for the ink, he's beautiful. Chad is a muscle-bound 5'10" with melon-fat arms and a chest so robust, it stretches his V-neck T-shirt to the breaking point. His powerhouse legs and bubble ass are barely contained by jeans so snug, they might as well be leggings. His waist is trim. His midsection has just enough extra to keep him from being *too* perfect. I covet his physique but savor a vindictive satisfaction that he's desecrated it with all this ink. I doubt he has considered what these tattoos will look like when he is seventy or eighty, when the taut muscle loosens and the flesh surrenders its elasticity, when the skin slackens to a leathery rind, turning the tattoos into sagging, crinkly cartoons.

"I need that pic. *Now*," Chad says in his best Anna Wintour. He storms back to his office. "We have deadlines around here, you know."

This is Tapestry, where a shirtless pic of a C-list celebrity qualifies as breaking news.

Friday, after work, I go to The Shed on Christopher Street. The Shed is dark, raw, and unrefined, but not grungy. Its floors and restroom neither gleam, nor disgust. It's your typical neighborhood gay bar. Cruising. A few drunks. Tank-topped, muscular bartenders (some straight). However, The Shed is atypical in one key aspect: its patrons are split almost evenly between Blacks and whites. An "interracial" bar, but rarely do the races intermingle. Mostly it's Blacks talking with Blacks while whites stand on the sidelines pining to be invited into the elusive world of the Gay Black Male. Sometimes that invitation comes; often it doesn't. Nevertheless, if you're white and into Black men—or vice versa—The Shed is the only bar I know of that caters to that.

I get my usual basil fresca and sit on a stool against the wall near the pool table. A game is in progress. I recognize one of the players, someone I met here a few months ago. A thirty-ish white guy with blond hair and a sunset-red beard. We talked for a bit that night. We seemed to enjoy each other's company—until I revealed the unthinkable: I live in Queens. Staunch Manhattanites revel in their superiority over the peasants who reside in the other four boroughs, although they make charitable exceptions for the gentrified parts of Brooklyn. In this way they are like fundamentalist Christians who think those who don't accept *their* version of faith are sinners. Unlike fundamentalists, staunch Manhattanites do not believe sinners should be saved or even paid attention to.

"Ok. Well. Nice meeting you," I told him when it was clear I'd worn out my welcome. "Time to head home."

"Why? You have to catch the last bus to Queens?" he said, and with a nastiness designed to stick.

My eyes leave the pool game and land on a bald, goateed white guy standing directly across from me. I smile. He smiles.

I look away. He looks away. I look back. He looks back. We engage in several more iterations of this ritual mating dance before he walks over.

"Ernie."

"Terrence."

He's forty-seven. A musician. Lives in Jersey City. Teaches music in Jersey's public schools. About 6'2" and slim. Ernie's thick goatee is speckled with gray. His dark bushy eyebrows are set low. They creep, slightly, onto his eyelids. With those low-set brows knitted together in consternation, Ernie looks mean. But when he smiles, his eyes open up. His cheeks plump out. His lips seem to burn a little redder. Which is why when he asks to exchange numbers, I almost trip over myself to comply. And why, when it's time to part, I give him a nice hug, a nicer kiss.

Ernie and I talk and text incessantly over the course of the ensuing week. We cover the arts, politics, the books waiting for us on our nightstands. We both love jazz and classical music. He composes music. Our conversations contrast considerably with those percolating through Tapestry: Lady Gaga's "awesome" new video. The guy on *The Bachelor*. The new "totally cool" dance bar. The newly discovered shirtless pic of Hugh Jackman.

On the phone one night, I tell Ernie I write poetry. He's intrigued. I like that. Poetry doesn't intrigue most guys I meet. It doesn't intrigue most guys.

"I'm trying fiction, too," I tell him. "I've written a couple of short stories. I can see writing a novel eventually. But right now, poetry is my thing."

"Can't wait to read it. You know what, Terrence? I love your voice."

"Why?"

"It's deep and distinctive and resonant. Authoritative, but soothing. You don't have an accent. It's like you're from nowhere. And everywhere. Your voice is beautiful. You're so articulate. Did you ever consider broadcasting?"

"No," I say, though I've been asked that before, and been told numerous times my voice is beautiful. I once worked in a call center and I know it was my voice that calmed and reassured even the most irate customers. I'm a little disturbed that Ernie said I was articulate. When whites say that of a Black person, it's often out of a sense of surprise. A sense that that Black person is the exception rather than the rule. Is that the way he means it? I don't know. I don't want to know. It's easier not to.

I want to tell Ernie I love his voice, too. The smooth tranquility of it. Its lush and slightly melancholic purr. But I don't, afraid he'll think I'm complimenting his voice only because he complimented mine. Instead I say, "You know what I like about you?"

"Tell me."

"I like that you call me and you text me and you email me without me always having to do it first. I don't have to do all the reaching out. You reach, too. A lot of guys don't. Most guys don't."

"I always will," Ernie says. "I promise."

This makes me nervous. It's too soon for promises. We haven't had a date yet. I don't know his favorite color, if he's a cat person or dog person, when his birthday is, if he likes his family. At forty-six I know better than to be beguiled by the promises of a man I've known for a week. Nevertheless, his promise sends me soaring.

We meet at Jupiter Diner on Christopher Street, not far from The Shed. We talk for hours. I confide that I hate my body. "From the time I was a little kid, people criticized my skinniness." I tell Ernie about the aunt who was sure I had worms. The coach who commanded me to stand in front of the class and said, *Gentlemen, this is the kind of body you* don't *want.* "Now I work for a company that idolizes the perfect bod above all else. I work out. I take supplements. Maybe I should apologize for not having better genes."

I hope I haven't turned Ernie off, made him want to flee Jupiter Diner and the self-hating, self-pitying, skinny Black guy.

"Your genes are fine," he says. "I can tell you have a cute bod. Even though I haven't seen you with your clothes off—yet."

I'm embarrassed. And pleased. And a little aroused. But Ernie starts to fidget with his coffee cup. He looks around the room, distracted, but not in an inattentive or rude way. His distraction looks like struggle. His bushy eyebrows crease in contemplation.

"Terrence, I need to tell you something."

I've heard this before, this prelude to some serious news that should have been shared sooner, before my hopes flew skyward. I steel myself, knowing one of three popular confessions is likely:

I have a boyfriend/partner/husband. If he tells me this, I will walk out without a word, without paying my share of the bill. I'll go home and go to bed and cry for hours or days or weeks or months over this man I've known for one week. I've done it before.

I'm moving to a faraway state soon. I'll be disappointed because he should have told me sooner, but I'll enjoy dating him while it lasts and try not to get attached. That attempt will fail miserably and, like the first scenario, I'll end up in bed crying.

I'm HIV-positive. This is, by a wide margin, the most popular and least frightening confession of the three. I'm negative, but have had boyfriends, one-night stands, and fuck buddies who I knew were positive. It doesn't bother me. I once met a guy on a Saturday night at The Shed and we left together. We had barely stepped into my apartment when he blurted, "There's something you should know. I'm positive." I replied, "OK. You have HIV and I have condoms. Make yourself at home. You want red wine, white wine, or seltzer?"

Now, in the half-moment before Ernie's confession, I sweat.

"I used to be heavy," he says. "Really heavy. Five years ago I lost 180 pounds."

He talks about being the fat kid in school. The pranks. The torture. Diets that didn't work or that he couldn't stick to. Reaching adulthood and getting passed up for jobs, how certain he is that his obesity was often the reason. Guys who wouldn't look at him, much less venture on a date. He almost cries recalling a night at the symphony when he had to leave because he couldn't fit in the seat. "The people around me—some were amused, some annoyed. *How dare he be fat. How dare we have to look at something so ugly and fat.* The next month I got a cash advance on one of my credit cards and had the surgery."

I am incredulous. Judging by his slim frame, you'd never know he'd once been atrociously overweight.

"And look at you now," I say.

"Yeah." He smiles. "Look at me now."

My place the next day. Ernie's coming. I'm fixing dinner: baked chicken, fresh asparagus, shrimp. I would normally include rice or pasta, but Ernie has renounced carbs. I gut the shrimp and try to temper my hopes and coax them down from their moon-high altitude. This always happens when I meet a guy I like: I get too far ahead of myself too fast. So fast I can't slow the momentum. So fast that, when disappointment arrives, I'm unprotected. Wisely or stupidly, I always try again. I hope Ernie is different. I think he will be. I always think that.

He's here. We hug as if it's been weeks since we last saw each other, instead of twenty-three hours and twenty-six minutes.

I pour wine, turn on the CD player which I've already loaded with jazz and classical, set to play randomly. The first selection is Dinah Washington's "Make the Man Love Me." I'm mortified that Ernie will think I'm trying to send him a message.

He takes a sip of wine, then sets his glass on the coffee table like a judge setting down a gavel. "I want to read your poetry."

"This very minute?"

"This very minute."

We go to the bedroom and sit at the computer, or rather, he sits and I kneel beside him, our arms spiraled around each other's shoulders. His eyebrows crease and uncrease as he reads. When he reaches the end of each poem, he kisses me. As he scrolls through the verses I think, *I'd like to live with this man one day*. Mel Tormé's rendition of "The Surrey with the Fringe on Top" ambles in from the living room, that foggy, velvety voice.

"Your writing voice is just like your speaking voice," Ernie says. "Resonant and soothing. From everywhere and nowhere."

He didn't say *articulate*. I'm relieved.

Our arms are still around each other's shoulders. We squeeze. I put my head on his shoulder. That evolves to caressing and kissing. I thought we'd have dessert *after* dinner, but I don't fight this. Ernie is aggressive, which I like. He maneuvers me to the bed. We undress.

I'm horrified at what I see.

I expected a slender body, and it is, but with blobs of excess skin budding around his pecs and bubbling his midsection. It streams from his buttocks, droops down his back. The excess skin is wrinkly, loose, devoid of elasticity or tautness. I touch it. It's gelatinous and squishy. It pours off his body like lumpy dough poured from a bowl.

I didn't expect a ripped body or six-pack abs or a high-definition chest. But I didn't expect *this* either.

Half-rough, half-gentle, Ernie propels me onto my back. His hunger heightens each second, but my arousal has withered. To reignite it, I shut my eyes, tight, tight, and think about how wonderful he is; how sweet and smart and cute; how he loves books and jazz and my poetry. I squeeze my eyes tighter, as if the strain might reconfigure my sight, redesign my visual perception so that I'll like what I see when I open them again.

I reopen them.

I see his body.

I can't do this.

I stop him, take his face in both my hands. I look into his eyes. "I'm sorry."

Flustered, jarred, breathless, he looks at me as if he doesn't understand: I've interrupted treasure and he can't make sense of why. And then he gets it. His eyes don't shift. His face and body remain still. But a heartsick air creeps up and envelops him. I feel it. If it had a temperature, it would freeze me.

He gathers his clothes—slowly, dazed—and goes into the bathroom. He closes the door. I hear him crying. The sound is tender, just like the tender man whom I have hurt. I sit on my bed and wait. When he emerges, we don't speak. We head to the front door as if—because—there is no other option. I have butchered the possibilities so ferociously alive only forty minutes ago. Our wineglasses, still full, dawdle on the coffee table. The apartment is flush with the odor of baking chicken. The music has changed. Leontyne Price singing the aria "Vissi D'arte" from *Tosca* in her dusky, opulent soprano.

Ernie leaves. Neither of us says goodbye.

I stand at the door for minutes, staring at it. Will I ever forget the sound of his crying? I fear it will crash through my head forever. I go to the kitchen and shut the oven off. I don't bother to take the chicken out. I go back to the living room, turn the music off, drain both glasses of wine. I sit on my couch. I put my head in my hands.

PAULIE

The pages explode with color. Ferocious reds and rusty browns and fluorescent yellows and saucy oranges and clear blues. Even the whites are bold and untamed. A jungle of color. It's almost too much to take in. One of my favorite Star Trek episodes has a creature that's so ugly, people go insane if they see it. That's kind of what this art does to me, but it's the beauty that makes me crazy. This artwork intoxicates me. I mean, I think it intoxicates me. I've never been intoxicated. I hear kids brag about getting drunk on alcohol they bought with fake IDs. I take sips of Mama's whiskey sours when she makes them, but not enough to get drunk. But if I were to drink a whole glass of whiskey sours, not just sips, and it made me feel good, made me soar—that's the feeling I have when I see this art. I soar.

The book is a collection of art by Myron Hillhouse. He's my very favorite artist. He calls himself a "neo-Renaissance" painter. He recreates ancient and classical stories, but with a racial twist: all of his subjects are Black. Black Moses parts the Red Sea as Black Israelites watch. Black Zeus sits on a gold throne in a white palace on the highest peak of Mount Olympus, clutching a thunderbolt in his fist.

I want to draw like this. I want to take fantastic tales and draw them to life, the way Myron Hillhouse does. I want to be like Myron. I want to push boundaries, color outside the lines. I want to do things I'm not supposed to.

"Hey, Crane. Still reading kids' books? Aren't you a little old for that?"

I turn my head. Ralph Knox's grinning, toothy face swerves into view. He wants to burst out laughing. And he would if the school librarians weren't so strict. Ralph wears tight parachute pants and a Mötley Crüe T-shirt. I hate Mötley Crüe. They're too loud. All heavy metal is too loud. But all the kids love it. Well, all the white kids. Culture Club is my favorite group. I love them. But I have to be careful who I say that to, because Boy George wears makeup. But so do the Mötley Crüe guys. They get to wear makeup but Boy George gets called a fag.

"Not smart enough to read real books, huh?" Ralph says. "Guess you prefer kiddie books with pictures. They're probably easier for you. Understandable for a guy who goes by *Paulie*."

And now he does laugh. A librarian, Mrs. O'Malley, is flicking through the card catalog. The massive shoulder pads in her pink blouse remind me of Krystal Carrington on *Dynasty*, or the gear football players wear. Not that I know or care anything about football. She shushes him and glares. The librarians at our all-boys Jesuit high school are very strict about quiet.

I don't respond to Ralph. I let him believe I'm reading a kids' book because that's what he wants to believe. I don't tell him that it's an art book and that it beguiles me. He wouldn't know what *beguile* means. There was a time I would have defended myself. I don't anymore. I just smile. My face gets hot. Not because I'm mad or embarrassed. But because Ralph's teasing is really a compliment.

People used to tease me for being skinny. My gangly, dangling arms. The sharp bones in my shoulders. My meatless legs. *Paulie Crane is nothing but skin and bones*, they used to say. Or *Paulie's last name is Crane because his legs are skinny as a crane's*. But last year I started working out. A lot. I'm not so skinny anymore. And everyone knows it. They see the muscles in my arms, in my budding chest. I make sure they see that. I wear my short-sleeve shirts a size smaller than my real size so that my pecs press against the fabric and the elastic at the armholes squeezes snug around my biceps.

I'm a very good-looking boy now. But when someone like Ralph finds a target, it kills him to aim anywhere else.

Ralph Knox is not good-looking. Ralph has pimples—raw, neon-red spots against a pasty white face, and a wild-animal mane of hair like Rick Springfield's. Ralph is fat. He has no business in those parachute pants. Nobody's told him tight clothes make you look fatter? I keep smiling for a minute, then I make a big show of shaking my head and going back to my book. I know he's furious. He hasn't gotten to me. I haven't let him. I'm better at this than he is. I wasn't always. It's a skill I've made myself acquire.

"Hey, Crane," Ralph says. I don't pay attention. "Calling Paulie Crane," he says, louder, and with some edge. He's desperate to get my attention. He hates that a former weakling he once made cry just ignores him, placidly. (*Placidly*. I think that's the right word.) Mrs. O'Malley shushes him again. Her shush is as loud as his talking.

I want to look up. Not for Ralph. For the boy next to him.

Drake.

Drake and Ralph are buddies, but he doesn't tease me or laugh at me like Ralph. He never has. He sits there and watches me. Drake likes me. He's never said so. Doesn't have to. That kiss behind the bleachers last month told me. Fumbling mouth. Sweat on his forehead. (Nerves? The Houston humidity?) What was he thinking? I wanted to know what he was thinking. I was afraid to ask.

Drake is everything a Black sixteen-year-old boy like me is not supposed to be attracted to: he's white; he's blond; he's male. Drake has sad blue eyes. Drake doesn't smile much.

He doesn't say much. He's always scared. Because he's slim and pretty, kids think he's "girlie." I don't. If it weren't for Ralph, he'd be more than an outcast. He'd be in danger. I've heard rumors that Drake does Ralph's homework and types his papers and helps him cheat on tests in exchange for protection. Ralph parades through school with Drake following behind, numb and confused, as if he regrets a deal he's made with the devil but can't undo it. With that blond hair and sad mouth, you'd think he was innocent. But I remember his fingers clipped on my nipples.

Drake hasn't talked to me since that day. But he's watching me now. I know he is, even though my eyes are in my book. How could he not? I'm a very good-looking boy.

"How old are you, Crane? Like, sixteen?" Ralph tries again. I'm so wrapped up in Drake, I'd forgotten about Ralph. "And still into kids' books?" He smacks Drake's arm. Drake flinches. "What a dork!"

Mrs. O'Malley has had enough. She marches over like a sergeant and hustles him out of the library. Ralph laughs the whole way out.

Usually Drake would follow him. I'm surprised he stays. He always seems tense when he's with Ralph. But now he exhales through his mouth and seems to sink an inch into his chair, as if he was propping himself up when Ralph was here and now he can ease down.

I'm glad he didn't follow Ralph out.

I put Myron Hillhouse aside, take out my sketch pad. I write the date in the top right corner of the page: April 17, 1986. I sketch Drake: the white neck (smooth, except for a couple of zits); the sad eyes; the lovely, trembling white hands. He's embarrassed at first. He blushes. He looks away, then back. Drake smiles. I've never seen him smile this big. He sits still, lets me sketch him. He's not blushing anymore. I sketch him for five minutes and everything is great. He seems to dig it. I wonder when we'll go back behind the bleachers. Maybe today? When will I get to hold his hand? Will it be trembling? I'll kiss it, place it on my chest to make it stop.

But Drake stops smiling. He glances around, nervous. He grabs his stuff and goes.

I miss him. I keep sketching.

"Paulie! Come here! This is the third time I've called you!"

I ignore Mama. I'm studying a painting of Jesus in my Myron Hillhouse book.

He has dark brown skin and a body like Hercules. Ripe pecs erupt off his chest. A meaty vein slinks down the inside curve of each bicep. His stomach is flat and perfect. He wears a white loincloth that slips down his waist slightly, revealing a fringe of black pubic hair. Light reflects off his skin. It's…iridescent. (I think that's the right word. *Iridescent*. I just learned it. I wonder if it's related to *incandescent*, and, if so, what the difference is.) A golden crown of thorns dazzles on top of a head with ropes of shoulder-length dreadlocks. Mischievous eyes, as if he's warning you away from sin and beckoning you towards it at the same time.

Sexy Jesus. It's why Myron Hillhouse is controversial, and why I like him.

"Desmond Paul Crane, Junior! Young man, get in here NOW!"

I thought if I ignored her, she'd forget she called me.

I gather up my sketch pad, but change my mind and take Myron Hillhouse instead. My father bought it for me because Mama wouldn't. He did it just to get to her. They broke up when I was nine. I don't care if they use me to slap at each other. As long as I get what I want. It drives Mama crazy when she sees me with this book. That's why I bring it to the living room.

"I expect you to answer when I call you," Mama says.

She's nervous and running around because Barrett, her boyfriend, is coming for dinner. She's in her slip and stockings and trying to do a million things at once. Checking on the food, straightening up, putting on lipstick. She has rollers in her hair.

She sees me with Myron's book and crinkles her nose. "You're supposed to be doing homework. Not playing with *that*." She puts the finishing touch on her lipstick with one hand and straightens the table place settings with the other.

"I finished my homework."

"I wish you were finished with that book. I still don't approve of that artist. Now I need you to watch your brother while I finish getting ready."

At that moment William, my six-year-old brother, flies out of the kitchen and into the living room with a toy airplane and rampages around the apartment, making zooming sounds.

"He's six. Why does he need watching?" I say.

Mama's shoulders sag. She half-smiles. "Sweetheart. Barrett's going to be here any minute. Be a good son and do this for Mama. Please?" She makes a pouty face. "Please?" She tickles my chin. I don't want to giggle, but I can't help it. She tickles my neck, my stomach, until I'm doubled over giggling.

"OK," I say.

She kisses me. She's almost to her bedroom when I say, "Mama, that charcoal drawing set, with the pencils and the charcoal block and the blending stick..."

Mama's head drops back as if begging heaven for strength. "Paulie. We've been through this. I don't have the money right now, but as soon as—"

I throw myself onto the sofa, bang Myron Hillhouse onto the coffee table, and fold my arms across my chest. "But you had money to buy William that airplane."

I got her. She can't defend herself, so she doesn't say anything.

"It's OK," I say. "Maybe Dad will get it for me."

She goes into her room. I can tell from the deliberate, soundless closing of her bedroom door that I've hurt her. I don't think I meant to. But I feel a sense of...delight. Not because I hurt her. But because it was so easy.

William is still zooming around.

"Captain William to the airport! Come in, airport! Ready to land! Ready to land! Alert! Alert! Plane landing! Plane landing!" He dashes through the house making airplane sound effects.

I hate him.

William is really my half-brother. We don't look alike. His

skin is light. Mine's dark, like Mama's. When we go places, people stare at Mama and me, like two dark people have no right to be with this beautiful, light-skinned child. Most times she ignores them. Sometimes she doesn't. *Good evening! How are you?* she might say to gawkers at a restaurant. *That fettucine Alfredo looks positively divine. Mmm. I'm sure you'll enjoy it.* Always polite. Always carries herself with dignity. I'm so proud of my mother.

William *is* beautiful. His skin is the color of light sand. His light green eyes are flecked with gold. His hair is a poof of brown, almost an Afro. We have William because Mama cheated on my father with a white man when we lived in Michigan. She doesn't talk about William's dad. But sometimes I hear her on the phone—and I have to put my ear to the door to make out what she says. I'm sure she's talking to William's dad. Sometimes she gets mad. Sometimes she hangs the phone up with a bang. She cries, sometimes. I can't stand it when Mama cries. I would do anything to make it so she doesn't have to. I think she cries because of money. She teaches psychology at a couple of community colleges. She says she doesn't make enough money, that rent and bills and the car payment eat up everything she earns and there's not much left. It makes her tense. It makes her worry. But if she hadn't cheated on my father, if we'd stayed in Michigan, maybe she wouldn't have to worry about money.

"Paulie!" William lands the plane on the coffee table. "Paulie! PAULIE! Mom told you to play with me."

Why do I call her *Mama*, but he says *Mom*? "She told me to watch you. That's different."

"But you're reading your stupid book. The one Mom hates because it's…obb-scene."

"Obscene is in the eye of the beholder."

William cocks his head. "What's that mean?"

"Go figure it out." I keep my face in my book. Little Willie can't stand being ignored. I feel his anger rise. I love making him mad. It's a game. And I'm better at it than he is. I let out a long, lazy, disinterested sigh. "I said go figure it out. Better yet: just go."

William is so mad, he's shaking. He's…apoplectic. (There's a word for you. *Apoplectic.*) I can guess what's next. And I'm right. William howls, clenches his fists, and flies at me. He's too slow. I slide out of the way and he crashes headfirst into the couch cushions. The cushions are soft. There's no way he's hurt. But he cries—pretends to cry. The "crying" sweeps up, up, up to a high-pitched scream.

Mama comes out of her room. "What's going on out here?"

She's dressed now. And she's gorgeous. Beige dress with short sleeves slit down the middle. A thin, gold-buckled burgundy belt cinches her slim waist. Tan four-inch high-heels give height to her five-foot-three frame. The rollers are gone, her hair styled in elegant waves. A string of pearls hugs her throat. Her skin: Brown and lustrous. (*Lustrous*: I love that word. What's it related to? *Luster? Lust? Illustrious?*) Mama reminds me of a Black version of First Lady Nancy Reagan: stylish, glamorous. I can't smell it from here, but I know she's wearing Chanel No. 5. Her favorite.

My mother is a beautiful woman. No wonder I'm such a good-looking boy.

William runs to Mama and hugs her. He makes sure not to bury his face in her stomach, but turns his head to the side so that his wailing isn't muffled. I know all his tricks.

"Paulie, what have you done to him now?"

Why does she assume I've done something? I mean, I *have*, but she didn't have to jump to that conclusion. I open my mouth to defend myself, but a knock at the door saves us from an argument. William stops crying instantly, magically. He runs to the door and opens it.

"Barrett!" he shouts.

Barrett scoops William up in his arms and barrels into the apartment. "Hey, tiger!" He nuzzles his forehead against William's. My brother giggles and squeals, then puts his arms around Barrett's neck, rests his head on his shoulder. Mama's excited to see Barrett. They've been dating over a year. She can't keep still.

She rubs her hands together, smooths her dress, primps her hair. I'm excited to see him, too, in his super-tight jeans and black boots and gray T-shirt with a deep V-neck that shows some of his mostly hairless, muscled chest. He and Mama kiss like young sweethearts. William is still in Barrett's arms.

"Barrett! Barrett!" William says as he squirms to the floor. "I'm a pilot!" He picks up the airplane and zooms again.

"Hi Bear," I say. My nickname for him. I extend my hand.

"Oh, come on, buddy. Gimme some love!"

His arms fly out wide and I fly into them and he encloses me in a fat hug. Hugs me so tight, it hurts. I ease into the pain, like I did behind the bleachers with Drake. Barrett is warm from the hot day. A little sweaty. When he releases me, I'm moist all over.

We sit down to dinner. Mama has made Barrett's favorites: pot roast, wild rice, and fresh green beans. Between bites, I sneak peeks at him. I call him *Bear* because it sounds like his name, but also because he's big. He played football in college. He has a bit of a belly. He has a goatee. He has brown hair, thinning on the very top. He's handsome. He's white. Another reason for intrigue when we're out together on "family nights." A brown woman, a brown teenager, a half-breed brat, and a white guy.

I like Barrett. I mean, I *like* Barrett.

I can't help it. I'm besotted. (I think I got that word from Shakespeare. It's a good word.) Yes. Besotted. With Barrett. My mother's boyfriend. Bear.

"Barrett, have you planned anything for the weekend?" Mama says.

William leaves the table—without excusing himself. Mama says nothing. She would if I did that. He gets his toy plane and comes back to the table.

"Tina Turner concert Friday," Barrett says.

"Ugh. I can't stand that woman. Can't sing. Prances around half naked. She needs to put some clothes on."

I think that's funny because Mama loves short skirts and halter tops. I can't help but snicker.

31

"How about Saturday?" Mama says. "Dinner? The four of us?"

"Sure. Somewhere cheap, though." He's mumbling, his head half bowed like a kid ashamed of himself. "Money's tight till next payday. Is Wyatt's OK?"

Barrett is an assistant manager at a furniture rental store. He and Mama joke that they're a perfect match because neither one of them make any money.

"Or," she says, "we could get together early, find some afford-able things to do, and make a whole day of it."

I set my fork down on my plate more loudly than I mean to. The metal clangs against the china. "Wait. The exhibit."

"What exhibit?" Mama says. She tries to sound innocent, but her girlish tone is too phony to pull it off.

"Myron Hillhouse. Saturday's the last day. You have to take me. You promised."

"Oh. That."

Barrett laughs. "Still disapprove, Justine?"

She jabs her pot roast with her knife. "I'm not the only one. That 'artist' has upset hordes of people. Controversy swirling all over the place. He does things just to get a rise out of people. A first-class provocateur. There were demonstrators in front of the museum when that exhibit opened." Mama's strict about table manners, but she's so worked up, she hacks her food to shreds, pops it in her mouth, and chews while she talks—a big, fat no-no that would put me in the doghouse. "*The Chronicle* did a story on him. Whites think he forces his own cultural misin-terpretations on traditional stories, but Blacks are excited to see traditional characters depicted as Black—until they realize Hill-house is white. Then they accuse him of objectification. Only Blacks should paint Blacks. That's their thinking, at least."

(After dinner I'll look up *objectification*; is it related to *object*? *Objective*? And *provocateur. Provoke? Provocative?*)

Mama's on a roll. "Art purists don't like him because he trashes the rules. Women say he's sexist because he only paints men. Religious people despise him because he's openly…," she

32

lowers her voice, "…homosexual."

Barrett stops chewing. His jaw tenses. I look at his ears. When Barrett's uncomfortable or embarrassed, he blushes, but only his ears. They turn bright crimson while the rest of his face stays pale. Like now.

"Mom, what's *home sexual?*" William says.

"Eat your green beans. Oh! And do you know why I have to take Paulie, why he can't go on his own? Hillhouse is so controversial, the museum won't admit anyone under eighteen into the exhibit unless they're accompanied by an adult. Now just try and tell me I should approve of this 'artist.'"

I roll my eyes. Barrett sees me. He smiles and rolls his, too. We're on the same page. I like that.

"Come with us to the museum, Bear?" I say.

"Sorry, buddy. Art isn't for me. I kinda hate it."

When he says that, something inside me crashes. I sip my juice to hide my hurt.

Bear reaches over and tickles William. William giggles. He looks at me, gets up, wiggles his way onto Barrett's lap, and wraps his arms around his neck. Barrett wraps an arm around my brother's waist. William locks eyes with mine, and snuggles even closer to Barrett.

I hate my brother.

I make my voice as cold as I can. "Since you're not going to the museum with us on Saturday, you should babysit Little Willie."

"Paulie, I've asked you not to call him that," Mama says, her voice dipping up and down in a sing-song. She won't tolerate calling him *Willie* or *Will* or *Billy*. But she's fine with *Paulie* instead of *Paul*. "And the museum will be a good experience for your brother. I'll make sure you get into the exhibit, and while you're admiring Mr. Controversy, William and I will see the other artwork."

I sneak peeks at Bear as we eat. At one point I stare, for minutes, uninterrupted. I want him to see me. He does. He smiles, and goes back to his green beans, Little Willie lounging on his lap. Bear looks up between bites. He stares back. His ears turn the most strawberry crimson I've ever seen.

I'm at school, sitting on a bench outside during a free period. I should be studying for a chemistry test, but I'm sketching Bear. I sketch him a lot. My pad is home to a collection of Bear drawings. I've drawn him sitting. I've drawn him gazing at the moon. I've drawn close-ups that capture the lines on his face, thin and fine as thread. This one is of his body, the way I imagine it naked. I've never seen him naked. That's frustrating, but inspiring, too, because I can draw him any way I want. I can muscle him up like a superhero. Or I can draw him realistically. His big, doughy body. The thick bluish veins sprawling through his forearms and his large hands. The pores in his face, tiny pinpricks visible only when our faces are so close we could kiss.

What would that be like? Kissing Bear? As I sketch him, I get sad. Because it's a terrible thing that he's never kissed me. But he's kissed Little Willie on the cheek and forehead. He burrows his head into Little Willie's chest and makes fart noises that make my brother squeal. He snuggles with him. Spoons his arm around Willie's waist. Why does my brother get to snuggle with Bear? Big kids need to snuggle, too. I have a right to snuggle with a man I care about. I imagine Bear's lips, chapped and rough, on my cheek. I imagine they're warm and leave a small moist spot.

Will Mama marry Barrett? What will that be like, having a white dad I'm besotted with? I want her to marry him. She was lonely before she met him. And now she smiles and gets excited when she knows she'll see him. Mama and I fight a lot, but I love to see her smile.

Will she marry him? I want to know. Sometimes the urge to know wells up. Makes me cry, or want to. Last night I was so close to asking her. I was in my room, working on this same sketch, and even just drawing him…it stirred something. I left my room, determined to ask her. But I couldn't. She was at the dining-room table, sitting up straight, her back a perfect line, her checkbook and a stack of bills piled in front of her. Her hands were in her lap. She didn't move, like something in a photograph, frozen in place. But then she leaned out of that frozen pose. She placed her elbow on the table, and set her forehead in the palm of her hand. Her perfect posture dissolved. Her shoulders rounded over, her weight slumped onto that hand. I wanted to hold her. But I went back to my room.

Barrett would be good to us. He'd love us. Is that asking too much? A nice man to love us? But would she cheat on him, like she cheated on my father, and bring another monster like William into the world?

Twelve minutes left in my free period. I'll fail my chemistry test. I don't care. I'm about to go back to sketching when I see Drake. He's on a bench on the opposite side, a little ways down. He's watching me. How long has he been there? How much time have I wasted not noticing? Free period's almost over. It's now or never. I wave him over. He hesitates, then comes and sits next to me.

"Hi, Drake."

"Hey."

His sad blue eyes flutter around. I want them to land on me. I want to take his hand and walk off this campus, our joined hands swinging like playmates.

Maybe things will go the way they did last month.

The school gymnasium. A pep rally. Cheerleaders from the all-girls Catholic school hopping around and bopping their hips and clapping and performing stunts with our school's male cheerleaders who, surprisingly, never get called fags. Me: hate sports, no school spirit, bored. Drake a row ahead and a little farther down, bored too, we don't stop watching each other, and maybe it's the crush of all these stupid, screaming kids, maybe their energy makes me bold, I don't know, but after a minute I spread my legs, place a hand on my crotch, push my tongue out. Five seconds. Ten. Drake doesn't blink. I stand, push through the crush, look back, he's up, he's following, I sneak out

35

of the gym, head to the track and the football field and the bleachers, I trust he's following but I don't know if he is until I'm behind the bleachers and he is, too. The kiss is clumsy, he hasn't done this before, or maybe he's nervous, but not too nervous to unzip me and take my dick in his mouth. His fingers tremble as he unbuttons my shirt, as he slides them up and down my chest and stomach, exploring, clutching handfuls of my pecs. His hands sweat, he pinches my nipples, the pain is soothing, like getting high, if I knew what that was like. Drake isn't nervous anymore. We kiss again. I'm not sad anymore and it's funny because I didn't know until now that I was. I don't care about being a very good-looking boy or sketching or Myron Hillhouse. I care about this, this boy with the sad blue eyes who likes me enough to risk everything to follow me behind the bleachers. But he stops. What's wrong? I ask. He steps back, he wipes his mouth, like something in mine was disgusting. He runs away. I'm left there, shirt undone, pants at my ankles, thinking: He wiped his mouth.

"What are you sketching?" Drake asks.

Is it to shock him that I show him the drawing of naked Bear burning bold on the paper? I expect him to flinch. He takes the pad, flips through the pages. He pays attention to each sketch.

"Paulie, these are really nice. I see you drawing all the time. But I didn't know you were talented." He's making me quiver. He's making my dick hard. "Paulie. About what happened. You know, the pep rally. I ran away because—"

"You wiped your mouth. And ran away."

I take the sketch pad back. My pencil scratches Bear's dick and fluffy pubic hair to life. It's the only sound until Drake says, "I'm sorry."

I'm ready to forgive him. I'm ready to kiss him. Until he says, "My mom and dad say it's mostly Black people who have AIDS. I was scared I might catch it."

His voice is shaking. He's shaking. He didn't say this to hurt me. But he's hurt me.

Tears fill Drake's eyes. But before they fall, Ralph Knox swoops down from out of nowhere, pimples gleaming. He clamps a commanding hand on Drake's shoulder. "Why are you hanging out with Paulie the Loser?"

I slam the sketch pad shut. If Ralph knew I drew naked men, the news would be all over school before the final bell.

Ralph struts away. "Drake. Geometry."

He doesn't check behind him; he assumes Drake is following. He's right.

Friday night. Mama's gone to her Black Republicans club meeting. Bear's at Tina Turner. I get to babysit Little Willie. He's on good behavior for once. He lets me enjoy *Dallas* and *Falcon Crest* without interrupting every five seconds like usual. I send him to bed when the shows are over and go to my room. I pick up my dumbbells for bicep curls, move to push-ups, and finish with a set of one hundred sit-ups. I strip off my clothes and look in the full-length mirror on the back of my bedroom door. My gaze scrolls quickly up to the top of my head before a casual glide back down, taking in my broadening shoulders, my pecs that get more sculpted every day, my trim, dimpled torso. I angle around so I can see my ass in the mirror. (At the mall a few weeks ago, I overheard a girl tell her friend my ass defied gravity. She was right.) My quadriceps are in good shape, my calves aren't. My one imperfection.

I put my briefs back on and go to bed.

I wake up in the middle of the night. The clock says two. I'm about to drift back to sleep, when I hear sounds from Mama's room. Moaning. Is she sick? I hurry to her room. The moaning continues on the other side of the closed door. It's joyous. I remember Drake's fingers clipped on my nipples, how I moaned at the pleasure in that pain. Now there's talking, giggling. Two voices, one deep, one airy. I know what's happening. I should go back to bed.

I don't.

I open the door a few inches. I peek in. Candles everywhere, on the dresser and night tables and the bookshelf and on top of the little black-and-white TV and on the window ledge. I face the foot of the bed. Mama lies on her back; her head dangles off the foot, legs splayed, bent at the knees and arched like pillars, arms behind her head, the pits open, freshly shaved, vulnerable. Barrett's on top of her, in her. He holds her wrists. There's something about the way he holds them. Something aggressive and possessive. And tender. His large white hands holding her small, dark brown wrists. Barrett moves, in and out of Mama, slow and mellow. (Mama has cassettes of a singer named Billie Holiday who sings a blues called, "Fine and Mellow." Is this what she's singing about?) The color contrast strikes me: his white body against her dark brown. I never knew white and brown together were this beautiful.

Barrett's face is above Mama's. Her eyes are closed, his aren't. It's the first time I've seen him naked. I almost faint watching the muscles of his large back. The jumbo mound of his ass. His thick, hairy legs. His bright, light, white skin.

Mama doesn't know I'm here. Barrett does. He sees me. I expect him to say something, alert Mama, shoo me away. But he gazes. With his face right above my mother's, Bear gazes at me, up and down. I'm in briefs. My dick is hard. Barrett gazes at my muscled, brown, young man's body.

I close the door, go back to my room, lie down. I begin to masturbate. I stop. Because if I do it, I might not dream about Barrett. I want to dream about him and wake up wet.

He's already at the table when I sit down to breakfast a few hours later. William's on his lap. Our eyes meet; Barrett drops his.

"Did you spend the night, Bear?"

"Don't be silly!" Mama says. "He just got here."

Pancakes and scrambled eggs and bacon for the guys. Yogurt and toast for Mama. Barrett feeds my brother like a baby. No one fed me on their lap when I was six.

Barrett hasn't spoken to me. I won't accept that.

"How was Tina Turner?"

"Great."

"Did you have a good time?"

"Yeah."

"Did she sing 'What's Love Got to Do with It'?"

"Yep."

Last night he ogles me while fucking my mother. This morning I get one-syllable answers. (*Ogle.* Not sure where I picked that up. Related to *mogul?*)

"What'd you do after the concert? Did your night end with a bang?"

And now, finally, as he's about to fork more pancake into Little Willie's mouth, Barrett does look. His ears go strawberry.

I'm good at this.

We go to the museum after breakfast. The ticket line is long, full of people like me who have waited until the last minute to see the Myron Hillhouse exhibit. I scan the lobby's lofty ceiling, marble floors and columns. A gigantic granite statue of an Egyptian pharaoh and his queen sits in the very center.

William fidgets, shifts his weight from one foot to the other, crosses and uncrosses his arms. "Mom, when's it gonna be our turn? I hate it here. I wanna go home. I want Barrett."

"You'll see him tonight, sweetheart."

Not like I saw him last *night.*

It takes an hour to get our tickets. I can't wait to see Sexy Jesus.

We pass the gift shop on our way to the exhibit. A bunch of toys on a display table catches William's attention.

"I wanna go in there," he says.

Mama nudges him. He won't budge.

"On our way out, sweetheart."

"Now!"

The shop has prints, art supplies, books, postcards of artwork from the museum's collection, stacks of Myron Hillhouse books, African masks.

And a whole toy section.

William rockets straight to it. Of course he sees something he wants—a red rubber ball. He locks it to his chest.

"Mom can't afford that today. Let's go. We have to get Paulie to his exhibit."

She tries to take the ball, but he won't let go. He whines, then screams. Mama tries to calm him but he drops to the floor—in the middle of the shop with the ball clinched to his chest—and throws a tantrum. He kicks and shakes his head like he's having a seizure. Customers and employees form a circle around us and our family drama. Some shake their heads. Jaws hang open. A white woman says to her friend in a Texas twang, "Mulatto children are the worst behaved." Her friend nods: "It's that mix of blood." Mama lifts William from the floor. He kicks and lashes out and shakes loose. At first I was annoyed, then embarrassed. Now I'm scared. Because I recognize something I've purposely provoked him to many times:

Rage.

William unleashes a barbaric scream and throws the ball with all his six-year-old might. It flies into an Oriental vase on a display table. The vase crashes and shatters. Everyone gasps. I'm horrified. Mama's horrified. Even William stops screaming and stares open-mouthed at the disaster he's made.

"Mom…I'm sorry."

His voice is tiny, like he's two, not six, an angel, not a monster. Mama shakes her head. She scowls as she peers down her nose at him. William hugs her, head pressed to her stomach. She doesn't hug back.

An employee hurries over with a broom and dustpan. An older Black woman. She cuts vicious eyes at Mama as she sweeps up the glass.

A white man in a suit comes over. He escorts Mama to the register. William stands next to her, quiet and cowed, not a trace of the mulatto monster. The man in the suit winks at him. "Well, little fellow, you've made quite a mess here." The same twang as those women. William stands tall. The attention energizes him. The man and Mama talk. She takes a calculator from her purse, punches the buttons. Gets her checkbook, writes a check, hands it to him. Gets a credit card from her wallet, puts it back, takes out a different one, and hands it to him. Mama takes out some cash and hands him that, too.

She heads for the door. She's . . . stoic. (*Stoic. Stowe? Stowaway? Style?*) She ignores the people still whispering about us. Are those tears? I want to kill Little Willie for making her cry.

He catches up to her, takes her hand like the sweet little boy he's not.

I assume we're going to the exhibit, finally. But she heads for the exit.

"Where are you going?" I say.

"Home. You can see the exhibit next week." She weaves through the crowded lobby. She holds her head up.

"Today's the last day! Mama, please!"

She stops. She faces me. Tears slide down her cheeks, mixing with her mascara, like she's crying oil. "Paulie. Let's go."

William stamps his foot. "Yeah, Paulie! Mom said let's go!"

Clutching Mama's hand like a favorite child. Yelling at me like I'm the bad son. How dare he? How dare she let him? This awful child she cheated on my father to give birth to. My legs give out. I plummet to the floor. I'm sitting on my haunches, head bowed, tears flowing as people surround us again.

Mama strides over. "Get up. *Get up*," she says, voice in her throat and dangerous. "Paulie, you'll regret this." She pulls her arm back like she's going to backhand me. It's suspended in midair, waiting for the right cue. The mascara is still spilling down, scarring her cheeks. She's hideous. She's not my mother.

The lobby is dead silent. Everyone is fascinated by the rowdy, troublemaking Black family.

A security guard approaches. Middle-aged white guy with a stomach that piles over his waist like it might slop onto the floor. *Splat.* "Ma'am, I'm gonna have to ask you to leave. Your family's creating a disturbance."

Mama gets in his face: "Fuck you." Without turning, her face still in the guard's, she says, "Paulie. Up. Now." But the shock of hearing my respectable mother curse pins me to the floor. She yanks William's hand and marches out of the museum.

The guard crouches next to me. His chubby hand grips my shoulder, gently. "It's OK, son. Come on. Get up. Go with your mom."

He helps me up, and walks me out of the silent lobby.

I lock myself in my room when we get home. I don't come out the rest of the day.

I don't answer when Mama talks to me through the door.

I don't respond to her apologies, her coaxing, her promises, her threats.

I lie in bed, hands tucked under my head, thinking how much I hate my brother. My half-brother. My half-white half-brother. But it's Mama I'm furious with.

Barrett comes over. They go to Mama's room. I sneak out of my room. Mama's door is partly open. I eavesdrop.

"Paulie was atrocious."

"I'm so sorry you went through that, Justine. I feel for the kid, though: That exhibit meant so much to him."

"If it hadn't been for his ridiculous exhibit, I wouldn't have been humiliated. I'm furious with William—I sent him to his room for the rest of the day and don't you dare go in there and play with him—but I can forgive him. He's six. Paulie should know better. He thinks he's so grown up and sophisticated. But in some ways he's more immature than William. I'm ashamed of him."

Back in my room, the ideas simmer, then boil. A plan takes shape.

I get up extra early the next morning and work out. Bicep curls until my arms are numb. A hundred and fifty sit-ups instead of the usual hundred. So many push-ups, my palms dent the carpet. It's one workout, but I see a difference. My chest blooms. My biceps swell. Skim your hand across my stomach. Do you feel the peaks and valleys?

I ask Mama for Barrett's number. It's the first thing I've said to her since yesterday.

"I've gotta get out of the house, Bear. Come get me." The *tick-tick-tick* of my watch fills the silence. "Please. I really need to talk." *Tick-tick-tick.* "If my dad was here…I miss him."

Tick-tick-tick.

"OK, buddy. I'll be there in an hour. Meet me at the car."

Barrett drives an orange Ford Pinto hatchback. The exterior is smudged with rust. Inside smells like stale gas. The air doesn't work. Yellowing foam sticks out of the ripped, dingy vinyl cushions. A Patti LaBelle/Michael McDonald hit plays on the staticky radio.

"How about that burger place on Westheimer?" he asks when I get in the car.

"I want to go swimming," I say. "There's a pool in your apartment complex, right?"

The veins in his hands bulge as they strangle the steering wheel. "I thought you wanted to talk." His ears burn strawberry. Patti LaBelle hollers. "How about a movie? I hear *Top Gun* is good. Or *Short Circuit*? Supposed to be pretty funny."

Tick-tick-tick.

"My dad used to take me swimming."

At his place, he says I can change into my swimsuit in the bathroom. "Who needs a bathroom?" I say. I strip off my clothes till all that's left is a white bikini.

Strawberry. Sweating. He looks at me, then away. Tries to smile. Looks again. Tries to look away again, and can't.

"Paulie …"

I set my body against his. Drape my arms around him, rest my head on his shoulder. He doesn't hug back, but I don't move.

Moisture spurts down my back. I assume it's my sweat, but it isn't: Barrett's crying. His arms wrap me. He holds me. He kisses me. Now that his mouth is on mine, now that his tongue is shimmering between my lips, now that I have him where I've wanted him so long, I'm not sure I can go through with it.

But I'm finally in Barrett's arms! I feel safe and sexy and loved. Barrett's dick is stiffening against my thigh. He wants me! Oh god! I *am* a good-looking boy! For the first time, I really know it's true—because Barrett thinks so. He wouldn't want me if I wasn't. I'd be crazy to walk away. Why should I?

Because Mama loves Barrett.

So do I.

Betray your own mother?

Yeah? So? She betrayed me. She betrayed Dad. Look what that got me.

Bear tightens his arms around me. He drives his mouth hard against mine. He really is a bear. Wild. Fierce. He's hungry. He's rabid. He might bite. I'll bite back.

He's driven me home. We sit in his car in the parking lot. The engine is running. I can smell the exhaust from the tailpipe. The air is so hot and humid, it's like we're sitting in a bowl of steam. Barrett's skin is flushed and red. From the heat, or is he still bright with release? I feel peaceful. And...euphoric. (*Euphoric. Euphemism? Eulogy?*)

Peaceful.

And euphoric.

I feel them, separately. But they whirl together, collide, exist one on top of the other, each inside the other.

Like Bear and me.

I place a hand on his thigh, rub it in circles. He's crying. He cried all the way here.

I've barely shut the door when the car screeches away, kicking up gravel and shooting exhaust as Barrett speeds off.

It's later that night. The phone rings. Mama answers it from her room. Several minutes later, she cries out. I didn't know the human body could hold a sound so raw and deep. Where in the body could a sound like that live? I go to her room. William has beaten me there. She's on the edge of her bed. She's sobbing so hard, she can barely get a breath, and when she does, her body heaves and jerks like it may explode.

"Mom? Mom?" William begs. She doesn't answer, so he shakes her, expecting a reply to tumble out. "What's wrong?"

I already know. That was Barrett calling. He won't call anymore.

Mama is hunched over, her face in her hands, wetness spilling out from behind them and crawling down her arms. William leans against her, his arms around her, crying, too. For once he's not pretending. He's comforting the most important person in our lives. It's the most loving thing I've seen him do. For the first time, ever, I feel something for him approaching love.

I've destroyed them. It's what I set out to do. I didn't know I would feel bad afterward.

"Mama. Please don't cry," I say.

She sits up. "Go back to your room, Paulie."

For the second time since yesterday, her mascara paints black trails down her cheeks.

I leave. William stays. Until now I couldn't admit that Mama and William have a bond that excludes me. It was too painful. They're a team. I'm the outsider. I always will be.

When I was little, I was lonely, but too shy to make friends. So I invented one. I named him Boris and I talked to him all the time. Boris was my best friend. Mama didn't like that I had an imaginary friend. Sometimes I got the feeling she was jealous of him. Did she feel left out? Like I do now? I wish I could talk to Boris now. I'd feel stupid: A good-looking sixteen-year-old boy shouldn't talk to himself. He shouldn't have to. Unless he's destroyed his own family.

I need to be busy. Sketching. Working out. But all I can do is sit on my bed. How will I live with myself? How will we live without Bear? What will we do without that wonderful man to love us? The peace and euphoria from earlier—I grab on to what's left of it, wrap my arms around myself, and hug it to my chest.

The phone rings. Maybe it's Barrett again. I'll talk to him. I'll change his mind. I'll beg him to come back. Did he tell Mama what happened this afternoon? I have to know. I snatch up the phone before it rings a second time.

"Hello? Bear?"

"Um…may I speak to Paulie, please?"

The voice is shy, sad. No one ever calls me. I don't have friends. "This is Paulie. Who's this?"

A drop of silence. "Drake."

It takes a moment to absorb. We haven't talked since that day on the bench. I'm tempted to spit something sarcastic like, *You can catch AIDS from Black people over the phone. It travels through our phone lines.*

"Drake. Hey."

"Hey. Um…how's it going?"

"It sucks. I destroyed three people's lives today."

"Oh. Well. I hope one of them was Ralph's."

"What happened?"

"I hate him," Drake says. "I told him today I'm not hanging out with him anymore."

Which will make Drake vulnerable. Without Ralph, the predators will eat him alive. "Will you be OK?" I ask anyway.

He doesn't answer.

The silence isn't awkward. It feels nice. Just us, me and Drake, wading in the silence.

"I'm really lonely, Paulie."

I turn out the light, climb into bed. "Me, too."

The dark is gentle. The night is a kiss. One of my favorite Myron Hillhouse paintings, *Morpheus*, depicts a Black man, naked and musclebound, surrounded by black night and stars. He holds the moon on his shoulders. He is the god of sleep and dreams. He is serene. He protects. He makes night calm and safe.

Drake says, "I know it's late. But do you…would you like to talk for a while?"

I lean against the headboard and cross my legs at the ankles. "Yes."

GIFT SHOP

"Bastard!"

And she slapped him so hard, she thought her wrist might snap. Her hand vibrated. Elliott barely flinched. He sustained his poise despite the sea of crimson gushing across his cheek. His lips tightened in an oily smile that was crafty, condescending, disgusted, and pitying all at once. The slap hadn't ruffled his signature sterling-silver hair—each strand was still coiffed firmly in place. Elliot cherished his hair as much as his suave $2,300 gray Armani silk-wool sports jacket. Nina wanted to slap him again.

"Don't be melodramatic," Elliott said. "It isn't at all attractive. I expect an adult conversation, to discuss my proposal reasonably."

"Well, I am soooo goddamn sorry to piss all over your shitty fucking expectations."

"Nina!"

Elliott despised foul language, thought it uncivilized and lacking propriety. Which was why, when they argued, Nina always pitched a smattering of curse words in his path.

She sat on the sofa and cried. It was alarming how quickly things could change. Only half an hour ago Nina had been reading, content with the world—or at least resigned that there was little she could do to change it—when Elliott swept into the house and, following a concise exchange of pleasantries, said, "Darling, I have a proposition," and then presented an idea so outlandish, she'd laughed out loud. A joke. It had to be. She'd been sure of it. But then she saw the steady set of Elliott's jaw, his mouth straight as a line on an architectural draft.

Elliot joined her on the sofa. He removed a handkerchief from his jacket's inside pocket and wiped her tears. "Nina. Darling." His tone changed to fluffy and teasing. It always did when needed to cajole her, manipulate her. Her guard shot up.

"What I'm proposing," he said, dabbing under her eyes, "is a natural extension of where our relationship has been headed for years." He worked his way down her cheeks, then set the hanky aside and caressed and primped her hair like a fastidious beautician. "Personally, darling, I think it's exactly what this marriage needs. Some—how shall I put it?—jazzing up."

How ironic. Elliott Dove detested jazz. So much so that Nina suspected he maintained subscriptions to the opera, symphony, and chamber music society for spite. Two months ago, friends had taken them to The Rum Closet—the ritziest jazz club in Lake Prince—to celebrate the success of Elliott's newest business venture. The evening featured a splashy three-course dinner and a live show by a famous saxophonist. Elliott didn't utter a word all evening, except to tell the friends that their money would have been more wisely spent on "tasteful" music. The Doves hadn't heard from them since.

He touched his cheek, where she'd slapped him. It was still a buoyant crimson and swelling. "This new arrangement could be very good for us, if you'd open your mind to it."

Nina snatched the handkerchief, blew a blotch of mucus into it, and stuffed it back in his inside pocket. Anger tiptoed across his face, so controlled that Nina would have missed it—the mild uptick of his eyebrows, his Adam's apple's quick quiver—had she not known him so well. He recovered quickly.

"Darling, we haven't been happy in some time." He attempted to take her hands in his, but she wrenched them away.

"We love each other, but it's been ages since we've been *in* love." He took her hands again and held on when she tried to resist. "Nina, look at me. *Look at me*." Elliott leaned in so close, their foreheads touched. "I want to be in love with you again."

Nina looked deep in his eyes, and laughed in his face. She cackled so loud, it hurt her own eardrums. Not simply because her husband's proposal was offensive or that he had the nerve to propose it in the first place, but because he possessed the charisma to almost pull it off. It would be easy to fall prey to his earnest handholding, his British-y Cary Grant accent, his liberal dispersals of *darling* (pronounced *dahling*). Add to that his ruthless handsomeness—undiminished at fifty-eight—and it would be understandable if a weaker soul than Nina succumbed. She laughed to celebrate that she hadn't.

Elliott Dove could drop a bombshell with the svelte ease of a gentleman. He just had. After ten years of marriage, he had announced tonight that he'd met someone new. A man. That wasn't news: she knew he was bisexual before they married. And she was well aware he screwed around. So had she. Theirs was an open relationship. The bombshell was that he wanted to move this new man into their home for a perpetual *ménage à trois*.

He may have billed it as a means of "jazzing up" a humdrum marriage, but Nina saw this for what it was: Elliott Dove loved pussy, but he loved dick a lot more.

"Imagine a pie chart," he'd said during their courtship. "One half blue, the other half pink. That's my sexuality, darling. Split evenly. Fifty-fifty." But blue had gradually—and insidiously—expanded until the pie contained only a sliver of pink, and he and Nina had retreated three years ago to separate bedrooms. Divorce had never been considered, much less discussed. The prospect of being alone at their age terrified them. A brazenly unsatisfactory relationship beat none at all. Nina was fifty-seven. As far as she—and much of the world—was concerned, an unmarried fifty-seven-year-old woman was a freak of nature, a failure.

"Where did you meet this new love of your life?" she asked.

"A sex app called Trick."

She wanted to laugh again. Proper, courtly Elliott prowling on sex apps? Nina was shocked. Then again, her gay friends insisted that the bars—once the bedrock of the gay male world and primary means of getting laid—had become relics. "Oh, Nina, honey," her friend Edward had once admonished, rolling his eyes at having to teach her the basics. "Meeting guys in bars is sooooo 2003."

"I won't allow him in my house," Nina said, staring straight ahead, her back straight as a telephone pole.

Elliott reached inside his jacket, extricated the sopping hanky. He held it at arm's length pinched between thumb and index finger, and walked out of the living room towards the half bath.

"Aren't you forgetting something?" he said, now out of Nina's sight. She heard the faucet running. "This is *my* house."

Damn. She *had* forgotten. Elliott already owned the house when they wed. At his request—insistence, really—she signed a prenuptial agreement forfeiting ownership. She had no real say regarding the house because, legally, she was no more than a highfalutin boarder.

"Then I'm leaving," Nina said. "I'll go to Pam's. I'll be gone before this sex-app slut moves in."

Dear god. How would she explain this to Pam? Her sister could be snobbish about failed marriages. Nina could already hear the lectures as Pam held up her own thirty-year marriage as the model against which all other nuptials were judged.

Elliott returned *sans* hanky and reeking of citrusy artisanal hand soap. "Then act quickly. He's moving in tonight. He's waiting in the car."

Nina was too outraged to respond.

"Darling," Elliott said, "I wish you'd reconsider. I love you. I know our marriage isn't perfect, and I want to correct that. An infusion of a new something—a new some*one*—will enliven us. There's nothing wrong with adding some flavor to a bland marriage. Jamie could be that flavor."

Jamie? Was she really going to be replaced by someone named *Jamie*? She would have expected a dignified name like Arlen or Nigel or Niles. Even something like Johnathan or Robert. But *Jamie*? She wanted to laugh again.

Elliott seated himself in the leather wingback chair. He slouched back, draped an arm on each arm of the wingback, and crossed his legs at the knee. He seemed relaxed, almost drowsed. "I want you to know what this dear young man has brought to my—"

"*Young*? You didn't say he was young. How young?"

"Um…yes…well…"

"Um yes well *what*? How young?"

"Twenty-five."

And now Nina *did* laugh again. A raw snarl that emanated from her gut.

"I fail to see what's so amusing," Elliott said.

"Let me make sure I fully comprehend what's happening here. You want me to agree to a three-way relationship with a man you met on a sex app who's over three decades younger than us. Is that what you're saying, or has something flown over my head?" He didn't answer. "Elliott?"

"Most people would think themselves inordinately lucky to have a twenty-five-year-old fall in their lap."

"I'm sure he's done a lot more to your lap than fall in it," Nina said.

Elliott hunched forward in the wingback until his face was in his hands.

Against her better judgment, Nina felt sorry for him. Felt sorry, period. She'd been struck when he acknowledged their marital misery. Elliott's embrace of the blue portion of the pie had been a factor. But so had she. Rigid and stubborn, she was often torn between her right as a woman of a certain age to be so and the obligation to compromise. She could not accept this proposal, but understood that she had contributed to its rise.

"Tell me about him," she said.

Elliott's head leapt up. He glittered with hope.

"I was in my office, positively entombed under a pile of paperwork. I wasn't having a good day. You and I had quarreled viciously the night before—one of our worst fights ever—about my comment to Lauren and Mackenzie about jazz being tasteless."

"It was incredibly rude, Elliott! They treated us to a lovely evening and you insulted them."

"Yes, darling, I've acknowledged—"

"I've called a thousand times to apologize and they won't pick up the phone."

"Nina—"

"Obviously they're screening their calls and they don't want anything to do with—"

"Nina! Darling, I need you to concentrate. So. The day after the fight, I was in my office having a dastardly day. I felt terrible about our fight, about making you cry. I hate it when I make you cry."

"It never stops you."

"Shut up!"

Nina loved getting under his skin.

Elliott took a breath to put himself back on track. "I wanted to apologize to you, but my anger and pride forbade me. My phone buzzed. Someone had messaged me on Trick. I read his profile, looked at his photographs. There was nothing ostensibly impressive about him. Yet I was impressed. Even messaging back and forth, he had an earnestness, a sweetness. Most men can't wait to send you their naughty pictures and for you to reciprocate. They're obsessed with finding out what you like to do in bed, and they exhibit an embarrassing lack of compunction explaining what *they* like in granular detail. Jamie was different. He didn't talk about sex. Well, a little, of course. But mostly he asked about *me*. Now, one could argue he was simply stroking my ego, and I'm sure to some extent he was. But I know it was more. We messaged back and forth all day, and that pile of paperwork subsided perhaps a millimeter. We met for dinner that evening. He's not gorgeous. He doesn't have a stripper's body. I wouldn't even call him handsome, exactly. Cute, yes. You know I'd never be caught dead with someone who wasn't at least that. He's horrifically naïve. Wants to be a writer. Of short stories. Not novels or history or political discourse. Short stories. Dear god, he told me he'd love to leave Lake Prince and move to New York and he hoped to find an apartment in Manhattan for less than a thousand a month. Can you imagine? He isn't the smartest thing ever dropped on Earth. Even so, there's something there. A genuineness. A decency."

"The boy genuinely wants your money."

Elliott owned five restaurants and a supper club in Lake Prince, as well as a stake in a handful of cushy real estate investments. He was self-made, had built himself from the ground up. That was one reason Nina loved him.

"So what?" Elliott said. "So what if money is part of the attraction? Or if it *is* the attraction? Nina, I'm too old to quibble about whether someone's intentions are one hundred percent noble. I want to tell you what made up my mind about him. You know I'm always forgetting to take my blood pressure medication."

"Damn it, Elliott. You're going to have a stroke if you're not careful."

"Yes, yes, I know. Will you please listen? Jamie called me the other day. He said, *Did you take your medicine, Elly? Take your medicine. And have you eaten? Elly, eat.* I invited him to live here that very evening."

"Really? Because he told you to take your meds?"

Elliott lunged from the wingback till he towered above her and shouted, "*You* didn't call me and tell me to take them. You never have."

He had kneecapped her, weaponized her wifely shortcomings against her. But that didn't hurt as much as the warm aura of love in his eyes when he spoke about Jamie. That hollowed her, suctioned all of the oxygen from her body, leaving her limp and empty.

Elliott stepped back, his hands on his hips. He was

statuesque and immovable.

"If your little gold-digging, sex-app boyfriend moves in," Nina said, "I move out."

She meant it as a red line. She hoped and prayed he wouldn't cross it. But Elliott shrugged off his statuesque posture—as nonchalantly as flicking lint—and said, "I'm going to the car to get him." He breezed outside.

This can't be happening to me, Nina thought. It was too absurd. She *felt* absurd, like a character trapped in a vicious comedy, a slave to the stage directions and plot spirals of a masochistic author. If only she could edit the scenes leading up to this, reverse course, write herself out of this farce.

Nina rushed upstairs to her room, yanked a suitcase from the closet, and set about throwing clothes, lingerie, books, and shoes into it. Overcome, she stopped. She sat on the bed and cried as she ticked off the miseries of the past decade that had led to this. In her head she created two categories—*Elliott's Fault* and *My Fault*—and assigned blame.

Loss of friends: *Elliott's fault.*

My loss of self-esteem: *Elliott's fault.*

No sex: *Elliott's fault, and my fault.*

Elliott's health: *My fault. Maybe.*

My always being in a rut: *Elliott's fault.*

My loneliness: *Elliott's fault.*

Jamie:… *My fault.*

She opened the drawer of her nightstand and removed a hand-sized, gilt-framed picture. Boyd, her son from her first marriage. He had died eleven years ago, age twenty-five. His absence was a bottomless cup—impossible to fill no matter how she tried. She had married Elliott a year after Boyd's death, thinking—erroneously she now knew—that the acquisition of one man would compensate for the loss of another.

A tear fell on the picture frame's glass. Fine man. The one and only good thing from her first marriage. In her swirling struggle for self-worth, Boyd had grounded her, given her the sense that at least she'd accomplished something, had brought something good into the world. If Boyd had lived, she wouldn't have married Elliott. There would have been no need. And if she hadn't married Elliott, she wouldn't now be suffering the humiliation of being displaced by a rent boy.

She heard footsteps and voices on the stairs. "Our room is down this hall."

"I should introduce myself to Nina."

"That isn't the wisest idea."

"I feel like I should."

"That room. Enter at your own risk, my boy."

Did this Jamie person really have the gumption to introduce himself? She ran to the door to lock it against this interloper. But she stopped. This was still her home. She was still Mrs. Elliott Dove. She'd face Jamie, call out his audacity. She wouldn't hide. She turned her back to the open door, girded herself.

A whisper of a knock on the door frame.

"Hi? Nina?"

She swiveled around, teeth and claws bared, ready to attack. But what she saw made her legs go soft before failing entirely. She thudded to the floor. Jamie rushed in, knelt beside her.

"Oh god. Are you okay? Should I get Elliott? Did you faint?"

"I'm conscious, so I doubt I fainted."

"Should I help you up?"

"That would be the thing to do."

He helped her to the bed, sat beside her. She looked at him, glazed-eyed, and couldn't stop.

"Wow," he said, "I've lived here five minutes and I've already been involved in a rescue."

"I wouldn't call it a rescue, exactly."

"I would. I mean, you fainted."

"It wasn't fainting, since I didn't lose consciousness. Remember? We covered that."

Jamie smiled, shyly, as if unsure who should make the next move, then remembering that he should. "Oh! I'm Jamie. I'm dating your husband. You know, Elliott?"

"Yes, I've met him."

"I guess this is awkward for you."

"That's one word for it."

"But this can work," Jamie said. "I mean, I'd like to think it could. If you, if you and me, if we, you know: me and you—and Elly, of course—if we gave it a chance. This *ménage à trois* thing could really take off!"

Elliott was right: the guy was an airhead. *Enough air in there to power a windmill*, Nina mused. But she was mesmerized.

Jamie was a ringer for her dead son Boyd.

He looked exactly like him. *Exactly*. Height. Weight. Hair. Face. Everything. If Nina hadn't known better, she would have thought she gave birth to twins and no one told her. Or that Boyd had been frozen and then reawakened exactly as he had been before his illness and death.

"Elly says you're moving out," Jamie said.

She could have spoken, but having Boyd next to her was magic. What if speaking broke the spell? She nodded, *yes*.

"Aww, shoot. That's too bad," Jamie said. A pout. "I sure hope you change your mind. Well. It was very nice meeting you. You're a nice lady. Real pretty, too. I totally see why Elly loves you."

"He told you that?" Nina said. "That he loves me?"

"Yup. All the time."

And he shuffled out of the room, hands in his jeans pockets, his head hanging down slightly, an *aw-shucks* smile puckering the corners of his mouth.

Nina watched him go, then knelt beside the bed where the picture of Boyd lay. She studied it a moment, then ran out of the room. On the other side of Elliott's closed bedroom door she heard the clink of belt buckles, tinkles of laughter, the dull thump of shoes hitting the carpeted floor, the whine of mattress springs.

She needed to finish packing, get to Pam's. But she didn't move. All she could think was, *Did Elliott really say he loves me? And Boyd. Boyd.*

A squadron of floating fish greeted Nina when she arrived at work the next morning.

They filled the lobby of the Lake Prince Museum of Fine Arts: dozens of balloon fish, pumped with helium and floating lazily through the high-ceilinged hall. Hand-painted in opalescent colors by a Famous Artist of the Moment, the fish were the museum's current special exhibit, titled *Stoneglass Fury/Exit Cypress*. Nina hadn't a clue as to the title's relevance. She'd given up trying to make sense of the so-called art the museum showcased. A sneaker exhibit had figured prominently on last year's roster. Nina had caused a mini scandal when a board member overheard her telling a coworker, "People are wasting their money: they could walk down the block to Foot Locker." She was punished with a write-up, her first in thirty years at the museum.

Nina dodged fish all the way through the lobby. She'd barely set foot inside the gift shop when she spotted Kit behind the jewelry counter, brushing his waist-length, dark, curly hair in broad, dramatic strokes. He fluffed and primped, angling his head this way and that to admire himself in the jewelry counter mirror. He neglected to offer assistance to the two ladies browsing the glass jewelry case he stood behind. Nina panicked: they could be secret shoppers. If they received poor service—or none at all—the shop's manager, Nina, would get burned.

She pounced. "Why aren't you helping them?" she hissed. "And brushing your hair in front of customers is inappropriate. Not to mention unsanitary. Come on, don't you know that?"

Kit plunked the brush on the counter. Static electricity popped in the freshly charged bristles. "Like, Orlando doesn't mind. He's seen me brushing my hair, like, a million times and he's never, like, complained."

You little asshole, Nina thought. Kit exuded the whiny, challenging air of a child telling his mom, *Well, Dad said I could*. His thin, high, airy voice and copious *likes* made him sound like a Valley girl. His black eyeliner and vegan-thin physique made him look like one. Nina had been so irritated, she'd failed to notice his clothing: black T-shirt with an Iggy Pop ironed-on graphic; faded denim vest; leopard-skin leggings made of a clingy, sparkly material. Leggings so tight, she peeked at his crotch to check for unsightly bulges. His outfit was appropriate for a punk rock thrift store, not a museum gift shop. But she didn't chastise him. She'd lost that battle. "Don't be uptight, Nina," Orlando said when she'd reported the neon-pink jumpsuit Kit had worn one day. "Kit's cool. The kid's got edge." Orlando wrinkled his nose at her. "And youth. We could use some youth around here."

The browsing ladies moved to a display of Chinese-style pottery.

"See if they need help," Nina ordered.

When she arrived in her office, she threw her handbag on her desk and herself into her chair. She logged on to her computer. When Grace, an ally in the membership department, IM'd to say good morning, Nina took the opportunity to vent.

> —I caught Kit brushing his hair at the counter. He's wearing leopard skin leggings.

> —lol they certainly like wearing interesting clothes dont they? better hope a board member doesnt see them brushing their hair. very uncouth!!! lol

Nina was confused. Who was Grace talking about? Was more than one employee behaving ridiculously? Then she remembered: Kit identified as nonbinary. He demanded everyone use *they*, *them*, and *their* as his pronouns. One day Nina was discussing scheduling with her assistant manager: "Kit's usually off on Wednesdays, but I'll need him to work it next week." He overheard and complained to Orlando, resulting in Nina's second write-up in thirty years: for "creating an intolerant, unkind environment" for her employees.

Nina contemplated confiding in Grace about the colorful events at home.

She had tiptoed to Elliott's bedroom as soon as day broke, put her ear to the door, and heard the *molto allegro* movement from Mozart's *Jupiter Symphony*. Elliott's favorite composition by his favorite composer. He always played it when in a triumphant mood. If she heard the *Jupiter*, Nina could be certain he'd bulldozed someone in a business deal or scored front-row seats at the opera. Hearing it was a sure sign that Elliott Dove had gotten what he wanted. He came downstairs as she washed her breakfast dishes. His maroon silk robe was covered with gold paisleys, the collar trimmed with fleecy black velour. The belt was cinched tight on a waist that was manly and wide but nonetheless trim. First thing in the morning and his hair was perfect.

"I thought you were going to Pam's," he said.

"I thought so, too."

She turned on her heel to leave, then turned back. "Elliott, I've shown you pictures of Boyd, haven't I?"

Elliott poured himself coffee. "When we first met, I believe." He put the coffee cup to his lips. He winced at the hot liquid.

"But not since?" Nina said.

"Darling, you've always been quiet about Boyd. I daresay downright secretive. In ten years, you've said hardly a word to me about him, which, frankly, I've never thought particularly healthy. In my family we were encouraged to talk about our grief. My dear mother—God rest her lovely soul—always said talking about it helps to bring about a sort of closure that can be comforting and—"

"Goodbye, Elliott."

Nina went about completing the tasks Orlando had assigned her, none of which she agreed with, especially his decision to remove the identifying category labels from the bookshelves.

"What if a customer can't tell where the Impressionism books are? Or they don't know where the Egyptian section starts?" Nina had asked.

"They'll ask an employee."

"Why should they have to? Why can't we just keep the damn labels?"

That earned Nina her third write-up: for "argumentative-ness" and "resistance."

She'd been resisting for two years, since a new executive director took charge of the museum. The new director despised the gift shop and was blunt about why: The merchandise appealed to women in their fifties. She ousted the longtime retail head—Nina's boss—and recruited the twenty-eight-year-old Orlando, who crowned himself Chief Merchandising Stylist. Orlando then purged the shop in a massive clearance sale, closed it for a month, and executed a full-blown renovation. The shop reopened sporting a minimalist design and upscale merchandise curated with the haughty eye of an aesthete. The core customers—women in their fifties—denigrated the new shop, hurling out descriptors like *precious*, *snooty*, *uppity*, and *pretentious* as if they were slurs. Nina agreed. But there was nothing she could do.

Just like with her marriage.

She removed the labels from the bookshelves, and thought about Jamie.

He couldn't look exactly like Boyd. It was impossible. Elliott had traumatized her, disrupted her senses so she simply *thought* Jamie looked like her son. Leave it to Elliott to give her PTSD. By the time she got home, the stress would have passed, she'd see and think clearly, she'd finish packing, she'd go to Pam's.

But when she got home, Jamie still looked like Boyd.

Elliott was at the dining-room table. Jamie stood nearby, a steaming tray in his hands, wearing her apron.

"Welcome home! I fixed lamb. Elly said it was your favorite."

It smelled delicious. Elliott and Jamie waited for her to do something. She needed to pack her stuff, get out, hire a lawyer wily enough to find a loophole in her prenup so she could get a share of the house. Most of all she needed to take her eyes off Jamie. But she didn't want to.

Nina sat.

"Awesome!" Jamie said.

Elliott was at one end of the long, rectangular table, Nina at

61

the other, like two board directors facing off. Jamie laid the tray on the table, disappeared into the kitchen. He returned with a platter full of vegetables and a bottle of Malbec. He poured for Nina first, the wine so deeply purple it was almost black.

"Elly says you like this a lot."

This *Elly* business bothered her. It was undignified. *Elliott* evoked sophistication. *Elly* didn't do her husband justice. Or was Elliott *their* husband now?

She watched Jamie slice his meat with care and place it neatly in his mouth. Boyd had always shredded his food and chewed with his mouth open, which drove Nina crazy. Boyd had been a strict vegetarian, snobbish about it, too. He never missed an opportunity to laud his own dietary habits and criticize hers. But what good was his superior diet? He was dead and buried, and Nina had before her a plate of succulent lamb cooked by his doppelganger.

She picked at her food, drank wine to combat the awkwardness. Elliott and Jamie did the same. Before long, they'd drained the Malbec. Jamie went to fetch another bottle. Even his posture and movements were identical to Boyd's. The way he led with his head, goose-like, the shoulders slightly stooped; his long strides; the long, swinging, gangly arms.

Jamie opened the new bottle. "Elly says you work at an art museum. What kind of art?"

"Flying fish."

"Oh. Like at Sea World. I always liked going there when I was a kid. The dolphins were awesome. So sweet. Maybe I'll stop by one day. We can have lunch outside. Do they let you feed the dolphins?"

It had to be an act. And yet sincerity was written all over him. He glowed with it. Nina could see his mind had raced ahead and he was already tossing mackerels into the dolphins' mouths.

"They don't generally let you feed the animals," she said, "but they might make an exception."

"Awesome!"

Against her will, a piece of Nina's resistance chipped off and rolled downhill.

She stopped picking at her food and ate in earnest. The lamb was flavored with something she didn't quite recognize.

"There's something sweet in the seasoning?" she said.

"Cinnamon. Gives it a kick. The trick is not to add too much. You want a hint of sweetness, but you don't want the thing tasting like candy."

"All things in moderation."

"OMG," Jamie said. "That's so true. And you thought of that on the spot. I wish I could come up with original things like that off the top of my head."

Nina and Elliott sneaked a glance at each other. Elliott mouthed, *See? I told you.*

"Paprika's good, too. For sweetness," she said, so quiet she barely heard herself. "I can't say I've ever been successful with cinnamon. It goes well with some meats—"

"—but not with others. Like certain poultries."

"Or fish."

Jamie wagged a finger. "Gotta disagree with you on that one. Cinnamon totally works on fish. Again, the trick is moderation."

Nina sat forward. "Don't you think it depends on the fish? I've had salmon seasoned with cinnamon and it's been divine, but with most other fish, it doesn't work. I think it has something to do with the chemical interactions."

"Baloney! Cinnamon works with any fish; you just have to know how to use it. I'll show you."

"Would you? I'd really appre—"

Nina caught herself. She quickly gulped more wine.

"Well," Elliott said. He'd followed their exchange by twisting his head right and left, as if watching a tennis match. "I'm a restaurateur, and yet it's thoroughly eluded me until now that cinnamon was so magical. What have I been doing all my life?"

They finished eating, remained at the table sipping wine. Nina stared at Jamie and didn't hide it. It was as if her son had come back. As if she were sipping wine with Boyd.

"Elliott says you write," Nina said.

"Yeah," Jamie said. "Fiction stories. I make them up."

"Hence the fiction moniker."

Elliott laughed soundlessly into his napkin.

Boyd had been a writer, too. Never fiction, though. He wouldn't have lowered himself. He considered fiction a wanton luxury of the privileged. He once caught Nina reading a romance novel and didn't speak to her for a week. A journalist and activist, he wrote advocacy pieces on gun control, animal rights, reproductive rights, environmental issues. He organized protest marches, got arrested at sit-ins at the U.S. and state capitols. He hated that she wasn't fervently ideological, that she rarely voted. Most of all he hated that she took up residence in the amorphous political center. Sometimes she thought he hated *her*. He ran a blog. Did the internet Powers That Be take it down when he died? She never read it, rarely read any of his work. Would it have been so difficult, she mused now, to read her own child's work? Maybe the blog was still live. Maybe she should find it.

"Have you finished any stories?" Nina asked.

"A few. They need polishing."

Nina stared at her plate. The juices from the lamb had congealed. She wrapped one hand around her wineglass, kept the other in her lap. Tears came. "When you're ready, I'd like to read them."

Jamie knelt beside her, wiped her tears with a napkin. Boyd never did that. Boyd would never have done that.

Nina watched Kit at the register and shook her head. Today's outfit: acid-washed jeans, dashiki, gray tuxedo coat with tails, black top hat. Although she disapproved, she had to acknowledge its quirky appeal, especially with his black eyeliner. East Village meets steampunk. It enlivened the shop, added character. The customers loved it—Kit received numerous compliments.

She was almost glad he wore it. Yes, *he*. She refused to think of him as *they*. She didn't care if she got written up again.

Her phone buzzed.

> —hi! hope ur having a #awesome day! pleeze pick up some #cinnamon on ur way #home. – j

She could have done without all the hashtags—they were nothing but millennial gibberish—but her heart twirled. It always did when Jamie texted, which had been often over the past two months.

She never went to Pam's. Evenings like that first one became the norm: Nina coming home and finding Jamie in the midst of preparing dinner; Elliott arriving soon after with an exquisite wine he took from one of his restaurants; or Nina finding them both in the kitchen in matching monogrammed aprons, frisky hands grazing each other's cheeks, arms, backsides. All that a prelude to leisurely dinners that Nina initially kicked herself for enjoying, but soon came to look forward to. Anticipation of those dinners was the fuel that buoyed her through her museum days, the armor that buffered her in her battles with Kit and Orlando.

They were the only true contentment she'd experienced in years.

During the dinners wine flowed, conversation flew, and laughter let loose. Nina enjoyed the laughter most. It was an elixir that transported her to an illusion of happiness. The more she laughed, the thicker the illusion became. The thicker the illusion, the more her stubbornness flaked away, and she surrendered, almost unconsciously, to the lunacy of a fifty-seven-year-old heterosexual woman sharing a house with her bisexual husband and his three-decades-younger boyfriend. Like a political spin doctor, she justified and excused and glossed over and downplayed and rationalized the arrangement. First by painting it as a necessary experiment in modern relationships, later by telling herself it was her only housing option, even though she

65

could go to Pam's or get her own place any time she wanted to. But she didn't want to. Because all the spin in the world couldn't disguise the reality: She missed Boyd, and Jamie was as close to him as she was ever going to be. Or the tragedy: This was closer to Boyd than she'd ever been.

It wasn't only about Boyd anymore, though. She liked Jamie, who stayed home all day, writing. Nina had once aspired to a creative career. She moved to New York City at eighteen to be an actress. She failed, returned to Lake Prince at twenty, and began a safe yawn of a career at the museum. She admired Jamie for pursuing his creativity full-time, even if the pursuit was subsidized by Elliott's money. Mostly, though, she envied him. Not for staying home—she could, too, if she chose, since Elliott had enough money to go around twice—but for being young. For not yet having a wormhole of a long past to drag him down its forever tunnel of regrets. For possessing an innate blank-slate resilience that enabled him to absorb change seamlessly.

She also envied his relationship—and his relations—with Elliott.

"Nina darling, would you like to join us?" Elliott had asked after that first dinner. He and Jamie were at the foot of the stairs, both luminous with wine. Jamie hugged Elliott from behind as he fiddled with the older man's belt. Nina declined, and kept declining each night he invited her. Still, she felt excluded. She would creep to their door and listen to them fuck. Their intimate sounds intrigued her. Laughter. Mumbled conversations. Kissing. Silence.

She longed to be close to Elliott again.

They *were* closer now. Before Jamie, Elliott hadn't smiled at her in years. Now he saw her off to work each morning with a hug that was more like a caress; welcomed her home with a kiss remarkably husband-like; and, sometimes during dinner—while Jamie blathered on, extolling the glories and nuances of cinnamon or paprika—leered at her with eyes that said, *Come hither*. After three years in separate bedrooms—and mostly having to gratify herself—Nina wanted very much to come hither. But she knew Elliott wouldn't venture to her bed, and his, although king-size, would be crowded.

The museum closed early for an event hosted by a major donor. Nina went home and found Jamie on the couch, typing on his laptop, wearing nothing but white briefs. The elastic waistband had gone slack, making the briefs sit slightly below his waistline. Why hadn't Elliott bought the boy some new underwear?

"Oh, hi," he said as he typed. "You're home early."

"*Hashtag* home. *Hashtag* early."

"You're learning!"

"Well. Trying," Nina said.

"I haven't started *hashtag* dinner. I was gonna text you later and ask you to pick up some *hashtag* oregano. We're having *hashtag* lasagna."

Don't push it, kid. Nina sat in the wingback. "I'll go out later and get some."

"Awesome. Elly's bringing a nice Prosecco."

Jamie scratched his crotch and resumed typing. He didn't seem embarrassed to be three-quarters naked in front of her. This was the first time Nina had seen him exposed. She was unsure what to feel. Jamie's face and height and general size were replicas of Boyd's, but was this her son's body? Nina hadn't seen Boyd without clothes after age twelve, not even in a swimsuit. She couldn't know if Jamie's body matched Boyd's with exactitude, if the sparse patch of hair in the crevice between Jamie's pectorals or the tight but not overly defined abdominals were copies of her son's. Frankly, she was perplexed as to what Elliott saw in him physically. There was nothing wrong with him, but Elliott could have any pretty thing who wanted a rich older gentleman. Surely there were young men with more muscular chests, heartier biceps, abs far more distinct than Jamie's. But then she recalled what Elliott had said about an early phone conversation, when Jamie told him, *Did you take your medicine,*

Elly? Take your medicine. And have you eaten? Elly, eat.

Nina was drawn to the physique's austere featurelessness, uncorrupted by fat or injury, unembellished by weights and workout supplements. Boyish and dewy. Spare. It projected a certain purity. Like a minimalist design, it possessed not one bit more than was necessary, and not one bit less.

"Working on a story?" she said.

"I sure am."

"What's it about? If you don't mind my asking."

"Oh no! Of course not! It's about a boy from a small town who dreams of going to the city to make it big."

Good god, Nina thought. *An abused and overused cliché if there ever was one.* One that she herself had lived through. But Jamie seemed wholly unaware of his idea's unoriginality. His eyes beamed as he typed; the tip of his tongue emerged at the corner of his mouth as he gave his writing his complete attention. His naïveté was stunning. His innocence beguiled Nina. He may have looked like Boyd physically, but the resemblance ended there. He had none of Boyd's hard edges or street smarts. None of the arrogance. Not one ounce of the high-horse disdain with which Boyd had often treated her.

Jamie was easier to be around than Boyd. Easier to love.

Truth be told, Nina missed Boyd, grieved for him still. But she didn't love him. She loved the idea of loving him, but she didn't love *him*. It hadn't always been so. She had loved him when she carried him in her womb, had been so vanquished by love that she would, at the most inopportune moments, simply stop and wrap her arms around herself and become completely still. And she had loved him for a few years, when he was a little boy. Loved his dependence on her, and that she was needed. But by age ten, he'd changed. Boyd became precocious, creative, and opinionated. He clawed away from her attempts to protect him, shelter him, pick adequate friends and activities for him. In high school he became contrary, embraced contrariness like a hobby. Anything Nina liked, Boyd decided not to, even if it was good for him. Any thought Nina expressed, Boyd purposely took the opposite tack, especially when she explained—always gently—that his opinion was flawed or outright wrong. And he was rude to her. Sometimes so rude that she couldn't respond and instead went completely still, as she did those months he'd been in her womb and she'd been overwhelmed by love. In college, Boyd eschewed her entirely, a revolt powered by a full scholarship at an elite journalism school on the other side of the country. Nina had discouraged him from attending. A journalism degree was for people who'd spend their lives working in bookstores, just as she was spending her life working in a museum gift shop after earning a worthless theater degree. Nina was left with nothing of him. And, left with nothing, what was there to love? There hadn't been anything to love after Boyd reached age ten. And none of it had been her fault. Not his rebelliousness, his rudeness, nor his decision to cut out of his life the woman who'd sacrificed so much for him, a fact of which she had frequently reminded him. She had been a good mother. Why couldn't he have been a good son?

Jamie made a final, dramatic tap on the keyboard, then banged the laptop shut. "Done! Now I'll get it published."

As if publishing a story was the easiest thing in the world. Nina couldn't help but smile.

"Jamie, would you like some warm milk with cinnamon?"

"Yes, please."

When Nina returned, she stopped cold. Jamie was sprawled on the couch as if lounging by a pool. His arms up and behind his head, his exposed armpits bursting with hair, legs spread wide. His eyes were closed. Nina's eyes went to his crotch. Through the white fabric, she saw the contours of a hefty penis resting flat at a pristine ninety-degree angle. Her hands shook, the cup of milk along with them.

Nina hummed as she flitted around the gift shop completing tasks. The volume on the sound system was too high—another of Orlando's "innovations." He claimed research proved loud music energized customers and made them more prone to spend money. Nina thought that was the silliest thing she'd ever heard. Was it Lady Gaga playing? She couldn't be certain. Today's female pop stars all sounded the same to her.

Kit was behind the jewelry counter applying eyeliner in the mirror. He struggled to keep his hand steady and became visibly frustrated with his continual blunders. He took a startled step back when Nina swooped in beside him and said, "Now I know why your eyeliner always looks off. Come here. I'll show you a trick to steady your hand. Pull up that stool. Sit down. Well, sit! Put your elbow on the counter, firmly. Good. *Now* apply the eyeliner. See? Resting your elbow on a surface helps stabilize your hand and keep it from shaking. That's a lot easier, right? Looks better, too."

Kit examined the results in the mirror. "Like, oh my god. It totally does." He turned to Nina. He seemed to hesitate between gratitude and suspicion. "Thanks." It came out like a question.

Nina resumed humming. Lady Gaga—or whoever it was—belted out a power ballad, if they still called it that. The voice roared up, higher and higher, wild and strident and screaming with emotion while the instruments shrieked to keep up. Nina wished Orlando would allow her to lower the volume, but that wasn't going to happen. So she hummed louder.

"Nina, are you all right, darling?" Elliott asked. "You're unusually quiet this evening."

Jamie had fixed hamburgers and french fries, the meat big and spicy and juicy on doughy brioche buns, the fries wedged large with the skins left on. Nina was shocked that Elliott would eat such common fare. He maligned burgers as the "food of the masses" and refused to serve them in his restaurants. Jamie was bringing him down to earth.

"I'm tired," Nina said. "It was crazy in the shop. I was running around all day."

Lies. The gift shop had been annoyingly slow. After Kit's

eyeliner tutorial, she'd retreated to her office and spent the balance of the day scrolling through Facebook.

They finished dinner. Nina didn't want the men to go up to their room. She dreaded the moment when they would climb the stairs and abandon her.

"Night, Nina," Jamie said. He kissed a cheek.

"Good night, darling," Elliott said, kissing the other.

Nina gazed at the sofa when they left. She imagined Jamie there, the elegant simplicity of his body in those slack briefs. She conjured up Elliott next to him, in designer underwear—of course—something sleek and scanty and too young for him, but that he looked spectacular in. Nina's face grew warm, then hot. She felt like swooning, so she sat on the sofa. Jamie's laptop was on the coffee table. She opened it. He hadn't password-protected it. Boyd would've put a password on his computer. Boyd had trusted no one.

She found the story Jamie had finished yesterday: "New Boy in the Big City."

He'd escaped. That was all that mattered. He'd waited till his father passed out exhausted from bourbon and the beating he'd administered to his son; waited for night to fall and, in the dead of it, under its cloaking mask, he'd sneaked out of the house (stumbled, really, burdened by bruises and blood and tears) and run to the bus station. By midnight, he was on his way, safe, hurt, anonymous. Two days later, he arrived.

A fresh start: that's what he was after. A blank book in which to rewrite his life, edit out the pain his ogre of a father had inflicted. But editing wasn't the same as erasing. He knew that. Fresh starts did not themselves heal bruises. He knew that, too. But a fresh start might be a newly opened window through which a crisp breeze might float, carrying kindness, and maybe even love, on its windy back.

Not bad. Not bad at all for a kid convinced he could feed

the dolphins at an art museum. She'd wanted to laugh when he said he'd get it published. She *had* laughed when Boyd said he wanted to be a journalist, laughed harder when he announced he was starting a blog he hoped would attract national attention. She'd warned him that big goals—journalism, successful blogging, Broadway—lived in the realm of dreams and were likely to remain there. Their relationship dried up at once. Nina had been shocked that a laugh could ignite such damage.

She wasn't laughing now. An epiphany was blooming, loosening the nuts and bolts and screws that clamped her together. She felt something soothing wash through her. This was how she felt when she used to get high during her New York years: calm, but invigorated. Certain. Head clear. Emotionally primed. Resilient. Curious. Ready. She exhaled, releasing oxygen until her lungs squeezed shut, then inhaled again, the new air, the fresh air, jamming her lungs to bursting. The fertile epiphany flowed, and Nina nodded in agreement with the voice deep inside that had been caged for too long and now began to throb. It asked why she hadn't been ready before, why she always resisted so strenuously. Nina kept nodding while a sentence from Jamie's story echoed through her like a bomb: *But a fresh start might be a newly opened window through which a crisp breeze might float, carrying kindness, and maybe even love, on its windy back.*

She slammed the laptop shut, strode up the stairs and straight into the men's bedroom. A single candle on the dresser lit the room. Jamie was on top of Elliott. She watched their undulation. She removed her clothing, moved close to the bed. Jamie noticed her.

"Elly," he whispered. "Look."

"Nina. Hello, darling," Elliott said. "Jamie, dear, hand me the remote control. It's on the nightstand." To Nina: "I'd get it myself, but I'm a bit constrained at the moment."

Jamie handed him the remote. A moment later the *Jupiter Symphony* swelled through the room.

The gift shop was busy the next day. Orlando had emailed a gigantic list of tasks. Nina had no idea how she'd complete them and help all the customers *and* finish her paperwork. Payroll was due today, too. She should have been stressed. But she stood in the center of the store while activity whirled around her.

Or was she the one whirling?

She had woken up that morning sated, simultaneously exhausted and replenished as she extracted herself from a tangle of arms. Now she hovered in the gift shop, seeing the world as if through gauze, yet comprehending it more keenly, more cleanly, than ever.

Orlando had hired two new sales associates. (*She* used to do the hiring pre-Orlando.) One scrambled to assist multiple people at once. The other struggled with offering gift recommendations at the jewelry counter. Everyone had to yell to be heard over the music, an enchanting electronica piece. Nina made a mental note to find out the artist. Kit, in the leopard-skin tights and a Hawaiian shirt and lei, was ringing at the register, the line of customers never-ending. Nina looked at Kit closely. She shook her head.

When it slows down, she thought, *I'll help them with their eyeliner. They've put it on all wrong again.*

THE GIRL'S TABLE

A spit wad just hit the back of my neck. Another one.

They been shooting them at me all morning. I told Mommy and Daddy 'bout how the boys be doing all kinda stuff to me—spit wads, tripping me, pushing me around in the bathroom. Daddy tell me to fight. He say better to get a bloody nose than be no sissy. But Mommy say I ain't got to fight, all I got to do is look them in the eye real serious so they know I mean business, and they'll stop.

I'm scared to fight them. But doing it Mommy's way ain't easy either. But I guess Mommy's way better than fighting.

Miss Carson at the board, teaching math. She showing us *greater than* and *less than*. I like Miss Carson. She got long, black braids all the way down to her waist. She wear a headband that match her dress—a African fabric, orange and yellow and light blue. Pretty colors. Pretty like Miss Carson. She explaining something to Melanie. Melanie always axing lots a questions. Miss Carson spend more time answering Melanie's questions than anybody else's in our whole second grade class.

Mommy say if looking them boys in the eye real serious don't work, I should tell Miss Carson. But I don't want to be no snitch. People be getting even with snitches.

Another spit wad.

My heart beating fast. I need to turn around, look them in the eye real serious like Mommy say. But before I can turn, I hear somebody whisper, "Pssst. Cedric."

Here my chance. I turn.

A spit wad smacks me right on my mouth.

Dean the one did it. He sit in the row next to mines, a few seats back. Dean wear a black doo rag. We ain't supposed to wear no doo-rag in the classroom. Miss Carson always telling him to take it off. He don't, though. Dean don't never listen. He smiling all big and bright. Like bright could hide the meanness. It don't. He holding a white plastic knife from the lunchroom. He been using it to flick the spit wads at me, putting them on the blade part, bending it back, letting go so the spit wad flies. Dean laughing out loud. Some of the other boys—his crew—they laughing, too.

"Is there something you gentlemen would like to share with the rest of us?" Miss Carson say. Nobody say nothing. Miss Carson shake her head. "Know what, guys? It's 1997. I'd think you'd act a little more civilized." She go back to explaining *greater than* and *less than*.

The spit wad stuck on my top lip. Like it's glued. I brush it off. I got to be careful not to lick my lip. I don't want to taste Dean nasty spit.

I turn back around and face the board.

"Pssst," Dean say. "Turn around again. Faggot."

When I turned before, I forgot to look him in the eye real serious. Ain't no use now. I stay facing front. I should be listening to Miss Carson, trying to see what she writing on the board. But I'm too busy crying and trying not to show it.

Miss Carson sending us to the bathroom to wash our hands before lunch. She sending us in groups. It's my group's turn, even though Dean's group still in there.

I don't wanna go in there. I wait outside the bathroom door. I'll go in when Dean come out. But he taking forever. I hate it when his group go before mine, 'cause he always in there real long. I'm scared to go in there. Maybe I'll skip washing my hands. Just today. But my hands got paint on them from art class. Mommy wouldn't want me eating with paint on my hands. And my hands is gross from wiping all them spit wads off my neck.

I go in.

It stink. Somebody in a stall doing number two. The sinks is rusty and brown. Some of the knobs on the faucets is missing. People done wrote names and curse words on the white walls and they got yellow stains. Some of them stains is wet. There's a puddle of pee on the floor. Dean laughing and messing around with some older boys from fourth and fifth grade. He still got that plastic knife, the one he been using to flick spit wads at me. He jumping at people with it like he Wesley Snipes in a action movie, and showing it off like that plastic knife's gold.

"Nigga, stop acting a fool," a fourth-grade boy say.

"Yo, Dean. You acting like it's a switchblade, dog," a large fifth-grader say. "That thing ain't even sharp."

"Yeah, it is," Dean say, like a wise guy. "I'm gonna prove it."

Dean strutting around. He tryna impress the older boys, tryna act big like them even though he small like me. Tryna act gangsta. The good thing is, he don't notice me. I'm drying my hands and thinking I'm lucky. I'm thanking god that Dean don't see me.

Then he do.

"Hey!" he yell. "Cedric! You gonna sit at the girls' table today?" He turns to the older boys. "Yo, this nigga sit with the girls every day!"

They laugh so loud, my ears rattle.

"Why you sit with the girls, yo?" the large fifth-grader say. He so large, he got breasts.

"He a faggot!" Dean say.

The large fifth-grader push me. I fall on the floor. The floor grimy. People be messy when they wash they hands and water spill from the sinks and mix with the grime and make the floor muddy and now it's on my hands and I just washed them. Somebody still in that stall doing number two. It stink so bad, I hold my breath.

"That true?" the large fifth-grader say. "You a faggot-ass?"

He tall. He wider than me. He got fat cheeks and two chins and a tummy like a big ball. I look up at him, like looking up at a mountain. He keep coming toward me. I scoot back. Now I'm close to the puddle of pee. I don't want that nasty pee on me. It get on me, my clothes be wet and stinking and when I get home I'll have to tell Mommy and Daddy why.

I got to get up.

I got to look him in the eye real serious, and he'll know not to mess with me. 'Cause I'm a good boy. And they shouldn't treat a good boy like this. If I look them in the eye real serious, they'll see I'm good. They'll stop this. Please, god, let them stop this.

I get up. But I don't look nobody in the eye. I run out.

Melanie and Paris playing with they dolls at the lunch table. Melanie's doll's Black. Paris doll's white. Melanie looking at Paris white doll, all jealous. Melanie wish *she* had the white doll. She want to comb that soft blond hair, have blue eyes smiling up at her instead a brown ones.

I want to play with they dolls. I want to hold them, comb they hair, dress them, tuck them in at bedtime, lay they pretty heads on the pillow next to me. I want to ax Melanie and Paris to let me hold they dolls. But I know better. Bad enough I sit at the girls' table. If kids see me playing with dolls, too, they be laughing at me even worse. Melanie and Paris my friends. They like me sitting here. But the boys don't. Even some of the girls be cutting they eyes at me, sucking they teeth. The boys sit behind us. Sometimes I hear *sissy*. Or *faggot*. Sometimes they whisper it. Sometimes they shout. We can sit wherever we want in the lunchroom, but the boys always hang together and the girls just want to be around each other. I don't sit with the boys 'cause I don't know how to talk 'bout ball and video games and rap. I don't like they nasty jokes 'bout girls' private parts and what grownups do in bed. I don't like how they always acting a fool and tripping people and flicking spit wads and calling people *nigga*.

Is something wrong with me?

Everybody think so. Daddy think so. He always ax, *Why you don't play ball? Why you don't stand up for yourself? Why you so skinny? Why you don't act like a boy supposed to act?*

I guess something *is* wrong with me. If everybody think so, if my own Daddy think so, then it must be.

"You want to trade dolls for one night?" Melanie say to Paris. Melanie looking at Paris blond doll like she want it so bad she could eat it up. Paris look at Melanie's Black doll and scrunch her face up. "Please, Paris? I'll be your best friend."

"Girl, you already my best friend," Paris say.

They trade dolls. Melanie all happy, but Paris frowning like she can't stand no doll the same color as her.

At least she got a doll.

I'm watching them, holding each other dolls, dreaming 'bout what it be like to hold one in my arms, pat the soft hair, look into the smiling face, thinking how a doll face look innocent and pretty. But I'm a boy. I should like football and basketball. But football and basketball ain't gentle. They ain't sweet. Dolls is. You can get hurt playing ball, but don't nobody get hurt playing with no doll. When you play ball and you make a mistake and the team lose, everybody be mad at you. They be yelling and cursing, talking 'bout how stupid you be for making them lose, for letting them down. But you can just take a doll to your room and play with it all quiet and don't nobody get hurt. Don't nobody feel let down.

I feel something on the back of my neck. It ain't no spit wad. Spit wads don't hurt. This hurt. Like somebody struck a match on my neck and then held it there and let it burn.

"Dean!" Melanie shouts. "What you doing?"

I turn around. Dean standing right behind me, grinning. He holding the plastic knife. It got red on it.

"I told them it was sharp," Dean say, looking at the knife like he proud of it. Like he proud a hisself. He walk away, toward the table of fifth-grade boys. They all looking my way. Dean walking like a big man. That large fifth-grader who pushed me in the bathroom, he high-fives Dean.

I feel the blood dripping down my skin. Like a insect crawling down my neck. I know it's staining my collar, the back of my shirt. I wipe my neck. My hand's red.

"We got to tell Miss Carson!" Melanie say.

"Girl, I ain't no snitch!" Paris say.

"Cedric's our friend. We ain't letting Dean get away with cutting our friend. Come on!"

Melanie take me by the hand and run, pulling me along. Paris come too, but she take her time. We don't say nothing when we get to the teacher table. We just stand there for a minute and wait for them to act like they notice us. Miss Carson ax us what we need. She look different from the other teachers 'causa her African clothes and her braids. The other teachers be looking at us all serious, like they don't like us interrupting they lunch. Melanie do all the talking.

"Let me see, Cedric," Miss Carson say.

Some of the teachers watching, shaking they heads. Some keep eating and don't pay us no mind.

Miss Carson been acting like she can't be bothered, but something change when she see my neck. She grab a napkin quick and tell me to hold it against the cut. "Press hard. Dean did this?" She been talking low and sleepy-like before, but now she loud. Her eyes all big.

"Yes, ma'am!" Melanie say.

"Yes, ma'am," Paris whisper. She looking at the floor.

I don't say nothing. I'm too 'shamed. All these teachers sitting here, knowing something wrong with me. I want to cry.

Miss Carson send me to the nurse. The nurse wipe the cut

with something that sting, then put a Band Aid on it. "Leave that on for a couple of days," she tell me. "Don't want that cut getting infected. Lord have mercy. I don't know why you kids treat each other the way you do."

She send me back to class. Miss Carson waiting for me outside the room. Dean with her.

"Well?" Miss Carson tell Dean. "Don't you have something to say to Cedric?" Dean don't say nothing. "You're not going to apologize?" Miss Carson sound mad. Look mad, too. Not mad like when the class be acting up and won't nobody be quiet. She a different kind of mad. She walking back and forth so fast, her braids is swinging. And her mouth all closed and tight. Like she so mad she might hit Dean. "You're already in trouble, young man. Don't think your parents won't be told about this." She put her finger in Dean face. It's shaking. "Now you apologize right now."

Dean look at me like I gross him out. "Why shouldn't I cut him? He just a boy who sit with the girls."

Miss Carson send him to the principal. I go in the classroom. It's noisy when I walk in, but it get quiet quick. Everybody looking at me. Melanie must a told them what happened. That girl got a big mouth. I sit at my desk. I know everybody behind me looking at my neck, the Band Aid on it. Miss Carson start teaching spelling. My favorite subject. But I can't concentrate. I keep thinking 'bout Mommy and Daddy and what they'll say when they see my neck and I have to tell them what happened. They'll be disappointed in me. *Why ain't you look him in the eye real serious?* Mommy'll ax. And Daddy'll say, *Why you ain't fight back?*

I'll tell them I ain't have no chance. I ain't see him coming.

FLUFF

I didn't answer the knock at the door. And I didn't look through the peephole because I knew who it was. But I stood at the door and watched two pieces of paper slide under it. When the sound of footsteps receded down the hall, I grabbed the papers. *Petition* and *Notice of Petition*. Bullshit legal jargon that meant the first steps toward eviction.

I hadn't paid a dime of rent in four months. My vulture of a landlord was circling.

I felt woozy. The eviction papers fucked me up. The heat made it worse. The A/C was off. I had to keep the electric bill down, especially since a final termination notice dropped the day before. I read through the eviction papers. I couldn't believe this was happening. Seeing it spelled out—all court-approved and official—I could've taken a shit in my pants. I collapsed on the couch. Before the papers slid under the door, I'd been mellowing out to Miles Davis's *Kind of Blue*, getting buzzed on the ebb and flow of his horn. I had jacked up the volume to get the buzz back when my phone rang. The ringtone was the old-fashioned kind from back when phones were just phones and not hand-held supercomputers that people couldn't put down. Because god forbid your eyes aren't plastered to a phone every second.

It rang again. "Hello?"

"Hey, bro." Guy's voice. It drawled, like he was strung out. "They're downstairs, in a blue Ford Explorer."

I grabbed the last of my cash and scrambled down the three flights of stairs. My dress shoes clacked against the dingy white-and-gray marble steps and shot noise all over the building. One old lady—the building was bursting with them—poked her head out of her door. She pinched her face up as I clacked by.

There was parking space along the curb, but the Explorer idled in the street. *Easier to make a fast getaway*, I thought. *If it comes to that.* Hogging the street like that, passing cars would have to crawl around the thing. Not a biggie. Happened all the time on these one-way streets in Queens. It was a polished midnight blue, windows rolled up and so darkly tinted, it was like looking into a black hole. The day was too gaudy and bright. The humidity was so thick, you could grasp it. I opened the passenger door, climbed in. My relief at the air-conditioned interior rivaled my shock at seeing a chick in the driver's seat.

"Hi there," she said.

"Uh . . . hey."

She must have sensed my surprise. "You OK?" she said.

"Yeah. This is the first time they sent a ch—a woman."

"Were you afraid you got in the wrong car?"

I was. I'd done it once before. Luckily this isn't some red-neck state with concealed carry laws, or I might have gotten my brains blown out.

"Can I get a hundred percent sativa?" I said. "Small baggie."

She pulled a black messenger bag from under her seat. Even with the dark tinting she was careful to keep it below window level. She was late twenties, early thirties. Black tank top, white denim pants, black sandals. Straight, shoulder-length brunette hair. Fruit punch-red lipstick, a little blush. Pretty. Young and plush and dewy. The kind of chick I liked to hook up with.

The engine droned, but was soundless enough that I could hear jazz crooning from the sound system. Could it be? A millennial listening to jazz?

"Impressive taste in music," I said. The smell of weed dangled in the air as she picked through the messenger bag. "'Pannonica.'"

"Banana-what?"

"The piece that's playing. It's 'Pannonica.' Thelonious Monk. He recorded it a couple of times. This version's from his *Brilliant Corners* album. 1956."

"What's a Thelonious Monk?" she said.

She should have just stabbed me. "Um . . . pianist. Composer. Jazz legend. Same level as Miles Davis, Basie, Ellington, Coltrane. Played bebop, hard bop, cool jazz and you don't know what the hell I'm talking about, do you?"

"I turned on Spotify and this was playing."

I didn't know what Spotify was. Probably some digital thing. I thought for a moment, then purposely stuck my foot in my mouth. "Yup. Love Thelonious Monk. Got all his CDs." I gave *CDs* an extra punch.

She stopped picking through the bag like someone had hit a *stop* button. "You still own CDs?" Like it was Nazi memorabilia. "Write checks when you go to the store? Get your mail by Pony Express?"

A concoction of astonishment and insults, topped off with a glob of disgust. The reaction I expected—and always got—when I said I own CDs; that I do DVDs instead of the streaming thing; that I subscribe to print newspapers and would rather die than subject myself to social media. Yeah, I know: it's the Twenty-first Century, the Digital Age, time to go green, blah blah blah. I get it, okay? But I need the CD booklet with the liner notes; the DVDs lined up on the shelf; the physical book they cut down a tree for. Look, if I can't see it, touch it, hold it, it doesn't exist. Yup. Old-fashioned. And I'm forty-seven, so to you I'm probably just old.

The chick pulled out a baggie. "That'll be fifty."

Stupid spending money on weed when I couldn't even pay my rent. I passed her the cash anyway. She passed me the baggie, never lifting it above knee level. I jammed it in my pocket. She was looking me over. Smiling and not trying to hide it. *Hmm*, I thought. *She wants me. Maybe next time I'll get a discount if I give her a little something in return.*

OK, you think I'm an arrogant prick. Normally, you'd be right.

But here's the thing: I'm not normal—I'm freakin' hot.

My biceps are so big and round, you'd think my sleeves were stuffed with soccer balls. I got pecs so large, my shirts barely hold them in. My ass is so perky, it's like there's invisible hands pushing up my cheeks. A big ol' bubble butt suspended in mid-air. You know how they draw superheroes? Sweeping shoulders, svelte waist, muscles busting out of those skin-tight costumes? That's what I'd look like if I wore a superhero costume. And my face—I'll just say it: I'm extraordinarily handsome. Capital *H* handsome. Movie-star handsome. Calvin-Klein-underwear-billboard-in-Times-fucking-Square handsome. It's understandable if you think I'm an egocentric jerk. But if you saw me, you'd know I wasn't lying.

The music had changed from Monk to Nancy Wilson singing "The Masquerade Is Over." From the set she did with Cannonball Adderly in '61. Nancy's voice tinkled like light fingers on piano keys.

"You're dressed like you're going somewhere," the chick said.

I was wearing dress slacks, shirt, tie, hard-soled oxfords. "Job interview costume. Got one in a couple hours. Haven't worked in a while."

"Not stopping you from buying weed."

"Sweetheart, weed is the only reason I've survived."

And the reason I was out of a job to begin with. I was a surgical tech till I got screwed by a random drug test. I'd smoked half a joint the night before during an unexpected hookup. They'd already tested me that week, so I thought I had some leeway. How'd I know they'd test me again so quick? Yeah, I get it: Random means random. But usually it was weeks between tests. It came up positive—of course. They fired me—of course. The state revoked my certification, and every time some jerk-off HR rep or stuffed-shirt hiring manager asked about it, I had to tell them. A year and a half later I was still unemployed, living on cold cuts and water, facing eviction, and in mortal danger of having to move back upstate to Tilton—my hometown—to live with my twin sister and her family. Enough to make anyone need a joint.

The chick kept checking me out and nodding, like she approved or something. Kind of weirded me out. She handed me a business card. "I know someone who's hiring," she said. The card had an address. No name. No phone number or email. Just an address.

"What's the job?" I said. Not that it mattered. I had an eviction notice upstairs.

She started the ignition. "Bye now. Have a good rest of your day."

Empire State Testing Corp. was in one of those monstrosities on 55th Street and Seventh Avenue in Midtown Manhattan. The kind of building that's all snazzy glass and steel, zig-zagging up sixty stories like some funky futuristic thing. Supposedly avant-garde, but really just overdone and full of itself. New York architecture has lost its character. Give me buildings made of limestone, with Art Deco spires and gargoyles instead of this modernistic horseshit.

I checked in at security and went to the thirty-eighth floor.

Empire State's receptionist was a Black guy with short dreads. He wore a set of big-ass headphones as he tap-tap-tapped at his keyboard. I waited, thinking he'd greet me or check me in or whatever it is receptionists do. But he kept tapping. I cleared my throat. Cleared it again, louder. Nothing. I waved my arms in front of him like I was flagging down an emergency vehicle.

"Hellooooo? Anyone hooooome?"

He stopped tapping, lifted his head in extreme slow motion, and snarled, "Is there something I can help you with?" Lips moved, teeth didn't. He didn't remove his headphones.

Two folks you don't piss off when you go to a job inter-view: the security schmuck in the lobby and the schmuck at the receptionist's desk. You do, you're screwed. I knew I'd earned a demerit with my waving routine, so now I had to make nice.

"Sorry," I said. "You probably couldn't hear me, so—"

"I was in the middle of entering information into a *Spread. Sheet*."

He over-enunciated it like it was something exotic. Pop music shrieked from his headphones, like he wasn't wearing any. Young guy, so he probably didn't know jack about jazz. Even though he was Black.

"I have a 2:00 interview for the test proctor position," I said. "My name is—"

"Check in on the tablet." He went back to tapping.

"I'm sorry?"

"Um ... the tablet?" He gestured at something with his chin. An iPad-looking thing clamped to the counter. "Enter your info."

"On that thing?"

"On that thing."

Self-service job interview check-in? Seriously? If you check yourself in, do you get to hire yourself, too? I entered my infor-mation, but had to ask him how to close out of the window.

"Um ... you press the 'save' icon?" he said.

"Sorry. My first time using one of these gizmos."

"Gizmos?" His mouth opened into a teeth-baring smile like an animal who just caught a whiff of blood. "Do you still use a flip phone, too?"

How'd he know? I love my flip. It's like the communicators on *Star Trek* that Kirk and Spock open with a quick snap of the wrist. Smart phone, schmart phone. Don't fuck with my flip.

I sat in the waiting area, opened my leather portfolio with my resume and a list of bogus references. I wasn't getting one from the hospital obviously, so I'd arm-twisted friends who owed me favors and coached them on what to say if they got called. I crossed my legs. Checked my watch. I wished I was home, stoned, listening to Billie Holiday murmuring sad songs, or Ella Fitzgerald scat-singing a storm of joyful nonsense. Billie matched my mood. Ella matched the mood I wanted.

I slapped the portfolio shut and thought, *Jeez. Another fucking interview.*

You know that old saying, *You don't truly believe something bad can happen till it does?* I believed it. I believed I could lose my job, my apartment, have to move back to Tilton. I knew it could happen. And now I spent my days smoking weed, listening to jazz, scrolling through endless job listings online, and schlepping to interviews where they asked, *Why do you think it's taking so long to find a job?* And always with a subtle tightening of the eyes, head turned slightly askew, mouth half-smiling to disguise their suspicion. Because what they were really saying was: *What's wrong with you? Something must be, or you'd have a job by now.*

"Hang in there," my twin sister had said on the phone earlier that week. "It'll be OK. You'll get through this."

"Think so?" I said. I told her about something I read—way before I got fired—about a flock of homeless people living in a state park in Jersey, and not your typical homeless. These folks had solid educations, serious career accomplishments. But they lost their jobs and failed when they tried to get back on track. One was some kind of research scientist. Published academic papers up the wazoo, lectured at universities. She was sixty—a non-starter in the job market. She moved to the park when the bank foreclosed on her house. If that happened to her, it could happen to me. Because I wasn't accomplished. I was a fuck-up.

"You are not . . . *that*," my sister had said. She hates cursing. "This will make you stronger. Remember the Laws of Attraction. Think positively."

That positive-thinking stuff is crap, but she was trying to help. I loved her for that.

"Come with me, please."

Someone had appeared next to me, out of nowhere. *Poof.* Young guy. Probably half my age. *Jeez,* I thought. *Another interview with a millennial.*

I extended my hand. He ignored it and strode out of the waiting area. I dashed after him, panicked I'd get left behind. Actually, he didn't stride—he swished. Ass cheeks smacking from right to left like a runway model. His pants clung to him like tights.

We got to his office and he slung out the first question as soon as he flopped in his chair.

"What are three adjectives you'd use to describe yourself?"

"Well . . . uh . . . um . . ." First question and I was already off-course. The guy made a production of sighing and drumming his pinkie on the desk as I fumbled and stumbled.

"Uh . . . dependable. Trustworthy. And . . . hardworking."

"How would other people describe you?" he asked.

"Uh . . . dependable. Trustworthy. And . . . hardworking."

I thought my joke would lighten him up. It didn't. I opened my mouth to give a serious answer, but he moved on.

"Do you think the customer is always right?"

"No."

The guy's eyebrows rocketed straight up. He yanked up a pen and chicken-scratched something on a legal pad.

He annoyed the crap out of me. His questions, his interviewing style. Everything about him. His swamped-in-gel hair. The curl—perfectly sculpted—hanging in the exact center of his forehead. The scruff grazing his cheeks and chin—too little for a full beard, but enough to mimic his generation's concept of "cool." Something about him struck me as artificial and—I don't know—premeditated. He was good-looking, I guess, but bland, so the premeditation fell flat. Like he was trying so hard to be hot when he wasn't. I could tell he was gay. It occurred to me: *Maybe he's being a dick 'cause he likes me.*

He kept banging out questions. "What are your five greatest strengths? What are your five worst weaknesses? Where do you see yourself in five years? Tell me about a time when you had an altercation with a coworker . . . Tell me about a time when you had to deal with a difficult customer . . . Tell me about a time when you were over deadline on a project and had to tell your supervisor you were having trouble getting caught up."

Part of me wanted to say, *How 'bout I tell you 'bout a time when I bitch-slapped an interviewer?* And part of me was terrified. Because I was fucking up this interview. With each answer, I fucked it up a little bit more. I was flailing. I had a barren bank account, an empty 401(k), an eviction notice, and I was flailing when I had no time and no right to. My life was sinking in quicksand and every effort to escape seemed to pull me in deeper. That was the worst part—the powerlessness. I didn't control my own damn fate. Recruiters, placement agencies, HR people, and hiring managers did. I was nothing but a puppet sinking in quicksand.

The guy put his pen down. "That does it. Any questions for me?"

I was pissed. At him for his asinine questions—they sounded like he got them from the Internet—and at myself for the asinine mistakes that landed me there. I leaned so far forward, my face was almost in his. My voice cracked. "Yeah, how about actually telling me about the job?" Tears rolled down my cheeks. I didn't wipe them away.

His jaw plummeted. He explained that Empire State Testing Corp. administered certification exams in various and whatever areas. The job: checking in test-takers, setting them up on computers, answering questions, troubleshooting technical issues, yada, yada, yada. Jeez. So much for taking tests with a number two pencil and a Scantron.

"Training takes two weeks," he said. "One, if you train full-time."

I didn't ask why it took two weeks—or even one—to learn how to give bullshit exams. I just wanted out of there, so when he started tapping at the computer—probably in a *Spread. Sheet.*—and asked if I could find my own way out, I said I definitely could.

Jeez. Another disastrous interview.

I left Empire State Testing and went straight to the address on the business card the weed chick gave me. Moving back to Tilton seemed inevitable. I wanted to be with my sister and my niece and nephew, get to know my brother-in-law who's a pretty cool guy. But I hated that town. I didn't have a single good memory of the place. Not. One.

My sis and me weren't close growing up. That's weird, right, since we're twins? I mean, we always got along. We didn't fight a lot or do the sibling rivalry thing. Everyone thinks twins are best friends, soul mates. My sis and me weren't. We didn't start getting close till college. She went to school near home, studied English. I majored in biology out West. Junior year, at Thanksgiving dinner, our dad asked what I planned to do with my "fancy college degree." I knew it was a trap, but I answered, "Go to med school, be a doctor." I waited for the trap to spring. My dad and mom looked at each other. Two tricksters in cahoots. My dad said, "Yeah. Like you're smart enough to be a doctor." He and Mom laughed so hard, I thought they'd choke on their Stove Top stuffing. Sis came to my room later. "Ignore them," she said. "They're mad you're turning out so good and they had nothing to do with it. You'll be a great doctor."

I didn't go to med school, but I didn't go back to Tilton, either. Now it looked like I had no choice. At my age.

Flowers flared out of window boxes up and down tree-lined Union Street in Park Slope, Brooklyn. Clinging, leafy vines scrabbled up brownstones. Couples in Birkenstocks pushed designer strollers with gurgling brats decked out in outfits way pricier than mine. Chicks in leggings traipsed by carrying yoga mats and vegan-gluten-free-sugar-free-caffeine-free-soy-mocha-chai-frappuccino lattes. Politically correct vegetables like kale—probably bought at the neighborhood organic food co-op or picked at the community garden—spilled over the top of some guy's recycled canvas shopping tote.

Jeez, I thought. *Stereotypical Park Slope bougies. Fuck me.*

I stopped in front of a four-story brownstone. The address matched the one on the card. I wanted to go back to Queens and smoke, put on some Nat Cole—his jazz stuff, not the commercial crap he did with orchestras and sappy strings. I'm glad they made him rich, but I hate those records.

I walked up the steps and into the vestibule. Young guy inside. Psychedelic tattoos scorched each arm from shoulder to wrist with a few scalding his hands. Bowler hat. Muscle shirt. Skinny jeans. Shaggy beard that reached his crotch. He leaned against the wall next to the buzzer panel. He was reading *Leaves of Grass* by Walt Whitman. He looked like Whitman with that beard.

" 'Sup, dude," he said. "Who you here to see?"

"I'm here about a job? A woman sent me." I showed him the card.

"Dude!" he said. "You got this from one of our best talent scouts. Go on in. Second floor. Talk to Personnel. Welcome aboard!" He startled me when he pulled me into a bro-ey half-hug. He pushed a button on the panel. "We got a live one," he said into the speaker. The door buzzed open.

The apartment doors were all closed. The pale lighting and tacky floral wallpaper crackling off the walls made the place feel ancient. That stale, bathroomy odor of ramshackle pre-war buildings wafted through the place. Whitman hadn't told me where to go once I got to the second floor, but I heard a voice from somewhere at the end of the hall. The scuffed wood floors creaked as I followed the voice. I peeked inside the room. Someone was shuffling through a file cabinet while chit-chatting on a phone wedged between shoulder and ear. A real phone. I mean, not a cell phone, one with a cord. A twirling coil that connected the receiver to a push-buttoned cradle with a wire plugged into the wall. Like I stepped back in time. The person on the phone was a Black drag queen with an afro the size of Jupiter. She wore red stilettoes. Without the heels, she was at least 6'5", *with* them, close to seven feet. Her mountain build—two parts muscle, one part flab—was wrapped in a clingy red dress that ended just above the knees. Her chest bulged out. I couldn't tell if it was a godly set of pecs, baggie man-breasts, or falsies.

She hung up the phone, kept shuffling through the files.

"You gonna stay in that goddamn door all fuckin' day?" she said. "Or is your ass gonna say somethin'?"

Her voice: a bear's growl. I was scared. I knew I should go. But I couldn't. I . . . I didn't want to. All I could do was think, *Wow*.

"Um…an associate of yours said you're hiring. Here's my resume if you'd like to . . ." I swallowed, "take a look."

Her hips bumped hard and slow as she made her way to me. She plucked the resume out of my hand, tore it in a million pieces, tossed the shreds in the air, and plopped her mountain ass on top of the desk. She gouged something out of her teeth with her finger, inspected it, and flicked it away. She primped her massive 'fro, crossed her arms, and glared at me. One hand cupped her chin, like she was contemplating, evaluating. She was so tall, her legs hung only a half inch from the floor as she perched on that desk. I couldn't move. I was in a trance. Dizzy Gillespie and Charlie Parker's "Salt Peanuts" played on a clock radio sitting on the file cabinet. My eyes went to her feet. The stilettoes were so red and licorice-slick, my mouth watered. The drag queen looked me over from head to chest to crotch to thighs to feet and all the way back up. She nodded, found my crotch again. Her mouth swelled in a lecherous smile.

"You older than what we usually hire. But you'll more than do. Mmm hmmm. Twenty-five bucks an hour. You start now. Go up to the third floor. Tell 'em Personnel sent you."

Just like that? No reference check? Background check? Credit check? Drug test? Oh, fuck, I hoped there wasn't a drug test. Paperwork? Tax forms? Hell, what about an *interview*? After the year-and-a-half drought that had ransacked my savings; after waking up bereft every morning because I had zero prospects and no health insurance; after suffering through interviews for jobs I knew I wouldn't get because I wasn't twenty-six;

after doubting my worth, my intelligence, my manhood; after going through all that shit, I was jumping up and down inside. But this was too good to be true. Too goddamn easy. I didn't even know what the job was. But I was broke. I was getting evicted. Twenty-five an hour wasn't much in New York, but enough that Tilton could go fuck itself.

"Tell me about the job," I said. "And the training."

She yawned. "Child, you want this job or not? They need you on the third floor. Go. Now."

The stairs creaked. Voices drifted down, and music. Pulsing, synthesized pop. Think disco balls, grinding pelvises. The sounds led to a bright room crowded with cameras, lights, cables, sound equipment, and a crew buzzing around a bed topped with two mega-muscular naked guys. A ginger. A peroxide blonde. Ginger on his knees getting done from behind by Blondie.

I stood in the door. The trance from before dazed me again. I came back to earth when someone barked, "Cut!" A five-foot-tall guy in a beret approached the bed. His pants were stuffed into black boots that came up to his thighs. He looked eighty. "An ice cream cone has more heat than this scene," he yelled. "What's the problem, guys?"

Blondie sat on the edge of the bed. He gestured at his lap. "I need some help down here."

His voice was deep and gruff and brutalized by a New York accent that wallowed in his mouth like lumpy gravy. He sounded like a garbage man from The Bronx.

"You'll have to help yourself for now," the old man said. He checked his watch. "And hurry. We're on deadline."

Blondie stood up. "I get a fluffer. It's in my fuckin' contract."

"We're understaffed. Personnel hasn't hired anyone yet."

"Den you pussies are in breach of contract and I'm walkin' off dis shit film. How do you like dem fuckin' apples? Whoa. Hold de phone. *Who. Dat.*"

He'd seen me. So had the crew. They wolf-whistled and ogled and smooched their lips. Told you I was freakin' hot.

"Did Personnel send you?" the old guy said. I stammered,

yes. "Finally," he said. "What the hell are you waiting for? Get over there!"

Was there equipment he needed me to haul? Sets or props to move? Lights to hang?

"Over...where?"

Blondie plunked down on the edge of the bed. Ginger plunked next to him. They looked at each other, then spread their legs at the exact same time, superwide dicks hanging like slabs of raw meat in a butcher shop window.

"Over here, sweetheart," Blondie said.

I was still in the doorway, half in, half out of the room. "Um ...Personnel said ... I mean ... I had asked about training."

Blondie and Ginger licked their lips. Blondie said, "Ain't ya heard of on-de-job training, sweetheart?"

My phone rang.

"Yeah?"

"Hey, bro. They're downstairs, blue Ford Explorer."

I wasn't dressed. I'd placed the order a half hour earlier, and gotten back in bed. I took my time putting on jeans, T-shirt, sneakers, sunglasses. I yawned in the elevator on the way down. I hadn't been outside yet. After lounging all day in the A/C, the heat sucker-punched me. The light. The bright. The swampy humidity. It hurt so good.

I climbed into the Explorer. The same chick was behind the wheel. I'd hoped she would be.

"Good to see you again," she said.

"Likewise."

And we snickered like the only two kids in on a crazy secret.

"Hundred percent sativa, please," I said. "Hundred-dollar bag this time."

"Big spender."

She passed the baggie. I passed the cash. She had that Spotify thing playing jazz again. Did she do that for me? It was

Dinah Washington's grandstanding 1955 version of "Come Rain or Come Shine." That woman was a fucking force of nature.

"You good with the job?" the weed chick said.

"Sure. It is what it is. Keeps the lights on. I needed to save my life. And I've done that."

I got quiet, looked out the window, took in my very nice neighborhood. I'd lived there eleven years. Hoped to be there eleven more. I scooted close to her—easy, so she wouldn't get scared—and kissed her cheek.

As soon as I got back upstairs, I loaded five Lester Young CDs in the stereo. My favorite tenor sax guy. Billie nicknamed him *Prez* because he was President of the Tenor Saxophone. I rolled a joint, sat in my bedroom window, smoked, surveyed the street, the apartment buildings, the bodega on the corner, the mailbox in front of the laundromat. Summer was out in force. Humid and brazen and ecstatic. People on the sidewalk fanned themselves, mopped their heads, schlepped umbrellas to deflect the sun. I heard the above-ground train rumbling, the drummer in the next building practicing, rap booming from a car stuck at a light. Smoky, delirious notes steamed out of Prez's horn. I was still in the window, still smoking, when the sun set; still there when the moon rose and the temperature quieted and the crickets started chirping. I pulled the screen up, leaned out the window, over the fire escape. I inhaled the night, inhaled deep, like I was in a field of wild and fragrant flowers.

YOU CAN'T DO THAT
TO GLADYS BENTLEY!

Gladys's fingers hopscotched across the piano keys, smashing out notes dunked in blues and dripping rhythm. It was her first song in her first set of the night. Her eyes hadn't yet adjusted to the dark club, the stage lights' blinding glare. She couldn't see a thing outside the stage, but her explosive smile blazed as she winked and waved and nodded at folks in the crowd like she could see every face. They were too drunk to know any better. Eight years into this craze called *Prohibition* and folks still acted like Saturday night was a bountiful Christmas with the ever-flowing, overflowing gift of bootleg liquor. Especially at clubs like The Clam House where Gladys Bentley reigned, enthroned at the piano, moaning raunchy, sophisticated, bluesy jazz and jazzy blues from 10 p.m. till dawn. Her clothes were as sophisticated as her music. No gowns or feathers or horsehair wigs for her. No, sir. Gladys manned it up—all 250 pounds of her—in sparkling white tux and tails, white shoes, and white shirt and bow tie, all of it crowned with a tall, cock-angled white top hat. Elegant white dressing elegant brown. She was dapper. Dashing. Debonair. At heart, Gladys Alberta Bentley was a gentleman.

Her backup band pumped and bumped, ornamenting

Gladys's piano, lifting it till the melody soared. Gladys moaned out some lyrics:

> *"My brown bowl's full of berries,*
> *They're ripe and juicy-sweet.*
> *My brown bowl's full of berries,*
> *They're ripe and juicy-sweet.*
> *I stick my fingers in my berries,*
> *The juice knocks me off my feet.*
>
> *Someone licked my juicy berries,*
> *Lord, child, I had a fit.*
> *Someone licked my juicy berries,*
> *Lord, child, I had a fit.*
> *When they said, I'll stop it, Gladys,*
> *I said, please oh please, don't quit!"*

Her eyes had adjusted now. The Clam House was packed. A cacophony of color. Whites up from downtown and Negroes down from Strivers Row and Sugar Hill. Men in suits and tuxes and chicks in flapper dresses with long strands of fringe drizzling off every inch. Negroes and whites mixed it up, drinking and breaking bread at the same tables. A Negro man fed broiled shrimp to a white woman, forking it into her buoyant mouth like feeding a child. A giddy group of Negroes and whites made toast upon toast with flutes of champagne like it was New Year's Eve. White-jacketed, black-bow-tied waiters cavorted through the narrow spaces between tables, noses high in the air, backsides swinging, one hand carrying a tray, the other perched on a haughty hip. A pair of white queer men on the east side of the room caressed each other's hands. On the west side a colored pair locked lips. A mixed pair frolicked at a table in the middle, white guy on colored guy's lap, colored guy's finger sunk in his boyfriend's mouth. Mannish women—*bulldaggers*, white and colored—cut loose in suits and ties; their hair straightened, short-cropped, slicked back; arms tossed around the backs of their chairs, legs spread as wide open as an invitation. Negro drag queens and white drag queens held court in royal, breathtaking regalia, made up like movie stars, styled wigs glistening, and those girls' gowns were more chic than anything on Fifth Avenue. The queens' curvaceous legs were crossed at the knee and swinging to the pulse of Gladys's piano. The Clam House. A rollicking Black-white island oasis set back from a brutal mainland. It was protected—oh so thinly—by the inhabitants' madness for sex, their craving to cross boundaries, and their determination to desecrate taboos. And all of it galvanized by the inhibition-lowering magic of bootleg liquor.

The place was packed all right. Every eye was glued to Miss Gladys Bentley. Of course. How could they not be glued to a 250-pound colored bulldagger smashing out blues? The spotlight made her smolder like a beacon in her all-white getup as she dished out bawdy blues.

> *"Got a deep hole in my floor,*
> *Come on, baby, don't you tease.*
> *Got a deep hole in my floor,*
> *Come on, baby, don't you tease.*
> *My hole is wet and muddy,*
> *Come on, baby, fill it, please."*

It was one of her naughtier songs, and that was saying something. The kind of Gladys Bentley tune that had got The Clam House raided in the past, and would again. Gladys scanned the crowd. A couple of Negro stuffed-shirts walked out, snooty faces painted with disgust. *Good*, Gladys thought. *Means I done my job.* And she'd done her job when the queers hurled their heads so far back with laughter, their chairs nearly tipped over. And when the drag queens nodded their royal heads, Gladys sat up a little straighter on that piano bench, proud to have earned their sage approval. Most of the white folks reacted like white folks usually did, squealing like brats electrified by a delightful terror in a Halloween haunted house. It's why they flocked to The Clam

House, why they braved their way to Harlem: to be scandalized by the antics of wild and exotic Negroes. It was Gladys's duty to give them what they came for. It was her pleasure to provoke. Offend. Shake shit up. Antagonize the stuffed-shirts. Challenge the highbrows who thought they'd seen and heard it all, disrespectfully let them know that there was no such thing.

> *"If you're good to me, baby,*
> *You can slide down my muddy hole.*
> *If you're good to me, baby,*
> *You can slide down my muddy hole.*
> *So stop clownin' 'round, baby,*
> *Come send Gladys to her soul."*

She pummeled the piano in an extended interlude, a transformation from bawdy blues to rip-roaring swing, from tongue-in-cheek irreverence to jazz combustion. Gladys closed her eyes. Whirled in the music. Got fucking lost in it.

She opened her eyes, caught sight of Clement, her assistant, hovering on the outskirts of the crowd. He wore a double-breasted suit with a three-cornered silk pocket square. A pink pearl stick pin pierced his tie. This conservative ensemble was a far cry from the glittery gowns he swished around in when he competed in the drag balls. He pronounced his name *Clay-MÓN*, like he was French, though his ass grew up in Waters Grove, Alabama, child number five of six in a family of sharecroppers. Clement was a *dicty*—an uppity Negro. When Gladys accused him of it, he'd plopped his hands on his hips, the way colored women do when they're about to set you straight. "Gladys," he'd said, "you got a Cadillac, a chauffeur to go with it, a $300-a-month apartment on Park Avenue, maids to clean your shit, and you callin' *me* a dicty? Girl, puh-leeeeeeez."

Touché.

Clement now looked straight at her. He slanted his head toward a redheaded white woman seated by herself. Gladys grinned. Fourth time this week the redhead had been here.

Always the same table, always alone, the only person sitting solo in the whole joint. Gladys knew she'd paid sweetly for the privilege—management hated seating anyone by themselves. The fewer patrons at a table, the less hooch to sell. The woman was young, pretty. In the turmoil of flapper dresses and beaded dresses and evening gowns, she stood out in her flat crepe frock and cloche hat. The frock was silk. She looked like a demure Lexington Avenue heiress, the kind of chick who spent her days lunching and shopping and going to tea, and evenings in her family's parlor being courted by some robber baron's plucky son. White gloves on her hands. A prim glass of sherry in front of her when everybody else was guzzling gin. She seemed light, weightless, in body, certainly, but in temperament, too. *Girl look like she ain't got no grit*, Gladys's grandma would have said. She was looking at Gladys. Hell, everyone in the club was, mostly with boozed-out eyes. But this girl's look was unvarnished. Soft yet unrelenting. *Fuck*, Gladys thought. *My favorite kind of bitch. The kind who knows exactly what she wants.*

And Gladys knew what *she* wanted, so she sweetened the raucous interlude, slowed it down, but kept the bounce. She returned the redhead's unvarnished look, and sang:

> *"Got me a pale, redhead gal with a rosebud 'tween her thighs,*
> *She lets me sniff that flower, the perfume gets me high.*
>
> *I stick my finger through the petals, push it deep and slow,*
> *Taste that finger after, it's sweet as sugared dough.*
>
> *I lick that redhead's rosebud, leave it sopping wet,*
> *I kiss her soft red lips—child, this shit's good as it's gon' get.*

She sang right to her. Didn't take her eyes off her the whole damn song. And the redhead never looked away, never lowered her eyes. By the end, the woman's soft red mouth had parted, not in shock, but in accord. Eyes still sealed to Gladys, she removed her white gloves. Tossed them on the table like trash.

Lit a cigarette. Blew a wisp of smoke that drifted about her like a gauzy veil.

Gladys's first set was over. She hefted herself up from the piano, walked to the lip of the stage, spread her arms out wide, and exploded that blazing smile again. The crowd awarded her a colossal ovation. Folks climbed on tables to cheer and whistle and thrash their hands together. She bowed and lumbered offstage, feeling the burden of her 250 pounds in her knees and feet. Good thing she was a pianist and could sit most of the night. Yeah, Gladys Bentley was fat. No one needed to tell her, but that never stopped them. Especially the critics, who lined up to slap her each time she opened a new act.

"The portly Gladys Bentley was in fine voice and did a large and exemplary job presiding at the piano, as always."

"Gladys Bentley, or *La Bentley* as she is affectionately known, costumed her ample, buxom frame in her signature white tux and top hat and delivered a weighty romp of a performance in her new revue. Her manly, contralto voice carried well in the large theater."

"Let's pray the piano bench at the Harlem Opera House has sturdy legs because the fatso, masculine, smut-singing Gladys Bentley sits on it for two hours each night as she assaults the audience with songs more appropriate for a house of ill repute than for respectable Christian people."

Now, accusations of obscenity and "smut singing" didn't bother *La Bentley* one bit. She was a smut singer of the highest order and proud of it. But the shit they wrote about her weight made her a child in Philly again, when her mother chastised her for being too fat, too much like a boy. "I already got sons," her mother would say. "Why can't you act like the daughter I want you to be?" When people asked if she read reviews, she said no. But she read them all, and every single one that called her fat made her want to cry. She fended off the tears by being smuttier, more outrageous, more offensive. More masculine. They didn't like that she was a fat, Black bulldagger? Fine. She'd say *fuck you* by shoving all three in their faces.

Clement leaned against the wall outside her dressing room, smoking reefer. His clipped eyebrows curved like rainbows. The tight backstage area drowned in the reefer's tangy smell. Clement smoked too much of that shit. He handed it to her.

"What you want me to do 'bout the redhead, Gladys?"

She inhaled a lungful and passed it back. A dab of lipstick stained the end. She didn't know if it was hers or Clement's. "What you think I want you to do, fool? Bring her white ass back here."

She went inside her dressing room, slammed the door, threw her top hat on the counter. She studied herself in the mirror. A spot of makeup smudged her collar. A mess of sweat soaked the fabric around the armpits of her tux jacket and was spreading fast. She looked good in her tux. Custom made to fit. Gladys studied her face. Her hair was straightened and cropped short like the bulldaggers out front. A sharp little widow's peak jutted from her forehead. Her short sideburns were trimmed neat. The hair at the base of her neck was a clean line. Mannish body, mannish hair, but a womanly face. *I'm kinda pretty*, she thought, *with my shapely cheeks, my smooth, brown, perfect skin.* She dropped into the makeup chair for a touch-up. Forty minutes till her next set. Gladys wore makeup onstage and off, just like she wore men's clothes onstage and off. Toni, her makeup woman, went to work.

"I listened to that last song," Toni said. She blotted the perspiration from Gladys's face before applying a fresh layer of face powder. "You *trying* to get the cops in here? That song was an open invitation to a raid. We ain't had one in a while."

"We could use one," Gladys said. "Good for publicity. White folks like coming to places that get raided. Makes them feel like they're doing something dangerous. If there's one thing white folks love feeling, it's dangerous."

"If you say so. Anyway, good crowd out there tonight. They love you."

" 'Course they do." Gladys tightened her eyes at Toni, like the makeup woman knew something Gladys didn't.

"Why wouldn't they?"

Toni ignored her. Toni had a pretty face and a pretty backside and big, delicious titties. But she was dark-skinned. Almost blue-black. In the Negro world, that was the mark of the devil. Toni was a singer and dancer, but producers—white and colored—insisted on *café au lait* skin and straight hair. With her mark-of-the-devil complexion, poor thing couldn't get a gig dancing at the tail end of a chorus line. This job with Gladys was likely as close to show business as she'd ever get. Toni wore the lightest face powder on the market. It made her look like a clown. Gladys felt sorry for her. They fucked around sometimes, usually when Toni was drunk and Gladys bored. But it was best to avoid sex with the women who worked for her, otherwise things could get . . . messy.

A knock at the door.

"Answer it," Gladys ordered.

Toni's hips rippled and rolled as she went to the door. They were wedged into a tight satin dress. Gladys recognized it: Toni's *I'm letting you know I'm available tonight* dress. Gladys shook her head. *Bitch, just tell me you want some. Fuck this coy shit.* Toni was out of luck anyway: Gladys was taken tonight. At least she hoped so.

Toni opened the door. The redhead stood there, left knee slightly bent. An unlit cigarette wilted from her right hand. In the light of the dressing room, Gladys saw just how red her mouth was, how vivid the contrast with her pale skin. A radiant strawberry bobbing on a pool of milk.

Toni sighed. "Another white chick, Gladys."

The redhead looked past Toni like she didn't matter. Her eyes were tied to Gladys's. That unvarnished look again. Something raw about it. Something tactless and barefaced. Shameless. Gladys was grateful to have had her share of shameless women, but none of them wore it as well as this one with her proper heiress clothes. The white gloves were nowhere in sight.

"Another white chick?" the redhead said. "Is this a common occurrence, Miss Bentley? White chicks showing up at your dressing room?"

Miss Bentley. Gladys liked that. "Come the hell on in, sweetness."

The woman floated into the room, her movements suave and fluid. She held up her unlit cigarette. "I'm out of matches."

Gladys swatted Toni's ass. "Light it for her."

Toni fetched a lighter from a drawer, banged the drawer shut, lit the cig. The woman inhaled deep, exhaled deep. "You can go now," she told Toni.

"Excuse you?" Toni said. "I gotta finish *Miss Bentley's* makeup."

"I'll do that. Go on." She heaved a patch of smoke in Toni's face. "Get out of here."

Toni was about to blow up all over her. Gladys acted fast.

"You heard her, Toni." She pointed to the door. "Get the fuck outta here."

Toni slammed the door so hard, the lights rattled.

Silence as Gladys and the woman sized each other up, predators priming themselves for battle. A full minute passed, then two. The redhead inhaled. Her chest expanded, her shoulders lifted. Gladys did the same. One more moment passed before they burst out in grinding laughter that left their throats sore and their eyes streaming tears.

"You may have to find a new makeup woman, Miss Bentley. I think I drove that one away."

"Child, please. She'll be back. I don't worry 'bout Toni's shit."

"What *do* you worry about?"

She pulled up a chair and lazily crossed her legs as if taking calm possession of the place. Gladys watched this performance and thought, *I worry about this right here: a beautiful woman laying claim.* This redhead wasn't the first woman—white or colored—that Clement had brought back here. But she was the first to try to command the lead in the game of pursuit. Gladys preferred to. It kept her in control and the women in their place. Both were crucial. Especially when the woman was white.

"I worry 'bout my makeup getting done before my next set

104

starts," Gladys said. "You told Toni you was gonna finish it. Hop to it."

The redhead stabbed her cigarette out in an empty coffee cup and went to work, picking up where Toni had left off.

"What's your name, sweetness?" Gladys said.

"Miriam. Miriam Townsend."

"Hmm. *Sweetness* fits you better. That's what I'm gonna call you."

Sweetness smoothed rouge onto one cheek, then the other. "Suit yourself, Miss Bentley."

"Always do. Call me Gladys."

"*Miss Bentley* fits you better." She put some red on her fingertip, fondled the coloring onto Glady's mouth. She stroked her lips. Top lip, bottom lip. Left to right. When she finished, she inserted her finger into Gladys's mouth and held it there. Gladys was tempted to bite, show this woman who was in charge. But she licked and sucked on it instead, flashing a little peek at what she hoped was in store for later.

"Why you came in here the last four nights?" Gladys said. "What's your story?"

"Can't I come hear the best entertainer in New York without having a story?"

Gladys was disappointed. She thought Sweetness was smart enough to know she didn't need to bullshit her way into Gladys's good graces—she was already there. Had been since she parted her strawberry-on-milk mouth and scrapped those white gloves. *The best entertainer in New York.* Flattery so hollow, it verged on insult. Nobody needed to tell Gladys Bentley she was the best entertainer in New York. She already knew that.

Gladys shook her head and stiffened her lips to a sneer. Sweetness, so tall with daring only moments ago, seemed to shrink. She flushed red as she sat back down and fumbled to light a cigarette. Crossed, uncrossed, re-crossed her legs, and none of it with the elegance of when she first floated in there. Gladys had humbled the bitch. All it took was a head shake and a sneer. *Gladys girl*, she thought, *you still got it.*

Gladys groaned a little as she hauled herself out of the makeup chair. She removed Sweetness's hat and caressed her bobbed hair, twirling the silken red locks around her fingers. People like Toni envied this hair. Gladys simply marveled at it. It lacked the strength, the endurance of most colored hair. Expose this silk to too much sun, it might change color. Imagine. Hair not hardy enough to keep its color. Sweetness closed her eyes as Gladys raked gentle fingers through her hair. She was tempted to grip a wad of it and give that head a sharp backwards yank. Sweetness's mouth trembled. She shuddered when Gladys touched her neck. Out front, the clarinetist spun out reedy notes that squeaked high and rumbled low; that scampered up the scale before shuffling back down; that widened in volume, then winnowed to a whisper, the kind of whisper Gladys made as she stroked the silk and spoke in Sweetness's pale white ear, and Gladys knew the girl was quivering, that she was breathing fast, that she was hearing that whisper like a roar.

"Sweetness, I'm gonna ask you one more time and one more time only: What's. Your. Story."

Sweetness rose. She primped her bobbed hair and put her hat back on. She smoothed her dress. She took a powder puff from her purse and patted her face. She took out a lipstick and spread a thoughtful, generous dose on her lips. She lit a cigarette. She shook out her shoulders and tossed her head. The bobbed red hair under her hat swung side to side.

"I'm from a prominent Fifth Avenue family," Sweetness said. "My life has been tennis, private schools, cotillions, sojourns in London and Paris. Two years ago, my parents married me off to Mackenzie Townsend of the Park Avenue Townsends. Perhaps you've heard of them, Miss Bentley."

Gladys loved being right. She had nailed Sweetness's background, in style if not in exact substance. And she *had* heard of the Townsends. Rare was the day that the mighty Townsends didn't get mentioned in the business or society pages. They were in oil. Barbarically rich, that family had more money than some small countries.

"Mrs. Mackenzie Townsend, huh?" Gladys said. "Sounds like one hell of a gig. Something must be missing, though, else you wouldn't be up in here putting your pretty fingers in this bulldagger's mouth."

Sweetness had smoked to the end of her cigarette. She lit another.

"Mack is a good man. Loving to his family, generous to his friends and the people who work for him. Quite handsome, too—one of the handsomest men you'll ever see. Before we married, he was the most desirable bachelor in the Northeast. I'm very fortunate. It may be difficult to believe, but things don't always work out this well for women in my world."

This shit was too good to be true. Gladys waited for the catch.

Sweetness dragged on her cig. "I do not love Mack and he does not love me."

She explained that the marriage had been negotiated by their families like the corporate merger it was. She shrugged. "It's simply how things are done in my world."

She offered an intimate peek into that world.

"Mack and I lead separate lives. We do things together, of course—parties and the theater and charity things and such—to keep up appearances. Appearances are everything in our world. But he spends most of his evenings with his mistresses. That's swell, because I spend most of my evenings with mine."

"Does he know?" Gladys asked.

"I don't know. And I don't know that he'd care. Before we married, he said I could do what I wanted as long as I'm discreet and don't cause a scandal. *No scandals and no police*, he told me." Sweetness got quiet for a spell. Her pale face darkened. "Mack doesn't hit me. But if I caused a scandal, I think he might. I think he might do worse than hit."

The room seemed to get cold. Gladys shivered. Sweetness shrugged again and stabbed out her cig.

"We don't have sex regularly, but he does fuck me from time to time. He has to. We're required to produce an heir, male preferably."

"It's what's expected in your world," Gladys said. "But you still ain't told me why you been in this club the last four nights in a row." She pointed at the girl. "And don't give me that best-enter-tainer-in-New-York shit."

Sweetness opened her cigarette case, but snapped it shut. "But you are. I've known it since I first saw you." She gave Gladys that soft, unvarnished look again. It evoked a vulnerability brusquely at odds with everything she'd done and said since floating into The Clam House that night. And something in Gladys stirred. Something rustled. A sparrow's feather at dawn. A flickering jazz phrase. Something quiet, but that might hold a holler inside it.

"A few weeks ago," Sweetness said, "some friends insisted on showing Mack and me a night on the town in Harlem. A night of jazz and debauchery in the wild jungle just sixty blocks north of us, they said. I wasn't terribly enamored of the idea, but Mack was game." Sweetness grinned. "You know, there are rumors that Mack has colored mistresses and an apartment in Harlem he fucks them in." The grin flared. "I wonder if there are any half-colored Townsend bastards running around. That would be something to hold over his head. I mean, I like the man, but you never know. Anyway. We came here, and saw you. I was fasci-nated. The white tux. The unearthly talent. That gorgeous brown face. That big, brown, unapologetically manly body. I sat at our table and fantasized about you in bed. Your big, brown body on mine."

The quiet thing that had stirred inside Gladys released its holler. It echoed inside her, made her heart warble. Gladys Bent-ley took pride in having had lots of women. But she hadn't loved a one of them. Never felt the rustling of a sparrow's feather or a jazz flicker. She worried she might be unable to love, which must be as harrowing as being unable to see or hear. Worse, she feared her big, brown, unapologetically manly body was unlovable. But maybe she and this woman could love each other. For the first time she thought it possible. Possible was sweet. It made the holler inside want to step carefully into the world.

Sweetness took out her cigarette case again. She extracted one and tried to light it, but her shaking hands made that impossible. "But what I love most about you," she stammered, "is that you don't give a damn about anyone's fucking expectations."

Sweetness started to cry. Gladys got up, took her in her arms, pressed the girl's head into her bosom. She let her cry a while, then went to the credenza, got a bottle of bourbon from a secret compartment in the side. She handed it to Sweetness who downed the liquor in gulps and growled, beast-like, as it sizzled down her throat. Out front, the sharp, burning yearn of the cornet heated the crowd. They cheered as the soloist ratcheted up the melodic fury to an unbearable degree. Gladys and Sweetness kissed, wet and sloppy, each face smeared with the other's makeup, lips and necks and cheeks bruised and bitten, the teeth marks red, angry, their desire for each other so aroused, they were almost crying.

The cornet eased. The kiss ebbed to a nibble. Gladys and Sweetness collected themselves. Sweetness adjusted her hat. Gladys noticed the girl's nails. They were painted a daring red. Like blood at her fingertips.

"I . . . I want you, Miss Bentley."

Sweetness was saying beautiful things. But women who said beautiful things might still fuck you over if the need arose. Gladys had learned to be cautious. Lots of women wanted her. The colored ones because she was famous, infamous, glamorous, rich. The white ones so they could act out exotic fantasies, learn firsthand if the primitive tom-toms of Darkest Africa drummed in Negro blood. Maybe Sweetness nursed those fantasies, too. Hell, probably did. But Gladys looked at the strawberry-on-milk mouth she had just devoured and decided to take her chances. She was about to tell Sweetness to get her ass over here for another kiss when they heard an uproar out front. Shouting and swearing. The thud of overturned tables and the shriek of smashed glass. Sweetness stepped into Gladys's arms like that was the only place in the world to go.

The dressing-room door opened. Clement leaned against the door frame. He yawned. "Here we go again."

"Where's my goddamn car at?" Gladys said.

"Usual place. Where you think it's at, girl?"

"What's happening?" Sweetness said.

Gladys took her by the hand. "Police raid, baby. Let's scram."

They escaped through a back door and into an alley. A colored chauffeur in a uniform held open the back door of a '27 burgundy Cadillac. Gladys and Sweetness climbed in.

"Miss Bentley, we forgot the bourbon."

"Miss Bentley don't forget nothing." She reached under the seat and dug up some bourbon, opened it, chugged deep, passed it to Sweetness who did the same. Gladys coiled an arm around the girl. Sweetness nuzzled, close and tight. The chauffeur gawked in the rear-view mirror. "What you looking at?" Gladys snapped, surprised he wasn't used to this by now.

133rd Street was chaos. Cars, horns, people laughing, people screaming, people drunk. Traffic dragged up the street in a listless prowl. The Caddie inched along in front of The Clam House. Police were loading whites and coloreds, men and women, queers, bulldaggers, and drag queens into a fleet of paddy wagons. Gladys saw Toni get scooted into one. She'd have to bail her ass out in the morning. Clement probably got away. Always did. The Caddie felt like the safest place in the world. Gladys wanted to stay there. She wanted to stay there a long time.

They kissed again, unaccompanied by any yearning cornet. The kiss erupted and would not be confined. Gladys pushed Sweetness back till she lay against the wall of the car. Her hand cruised under Sweetness's dress. She clawed off her underwear, parted her legs, and shoved her face in the plushness. She didn't give a shit that the chauffeur could see them or hear Sweetness moaning. *He better not say a goddamn word*, Gladys thought. *Not one god—*

Something bashed the window on Gladys's side. Glass hurtled into the car. A jagged hole appeared in the window. An eye peered through it. A blunt instrument hacked at the remaining glass, spraying shards on the women as both screamed. A cop's head appeared. He was red-faced and furious, clutching a billy club. He reached through what was once the window, latched onto a struggling Gladys, and tried to pull her out.

He looked behind him and yelled, "You two! Get over here!"

Two cops rushed over. They were Negroes. They yanked the car door open and dragged Gladys out as she writhed and flailed and wrestled. The door on Sweetness's side opened, too, but she was helped rather than dragged from the car. "It's all right, miss," a white cop said. His tone was cool and soothing, as if calming a traumatized child. "He'll be punished for what he did to you." He placed his hand under her chin. "You have our word."

"What *he* did?" Sweetness said. "No, you've got it all wrong. He—I can . . . I can explain."

"Tell them, Sweetness!" Gladys shouted. "Straighten this shit out!"

But Sweetness didn't. Sweetness looked like she was in a daze. Sweetness looked terrified. Sweetness saw the cops, the paddy wagons, the crowd swelling the sidewalks along 133rd. Sweetness was Mrs. Mackenzie Townsend of the Park Avenue Townsends. Sweetness had expectations to fulfill in her world. In Sweetness's world scandal was not allowed. Sweetness's eyes landed on Gladys. Sweetness turned to the soothing white cop. Sweetness said, "He raped me." Sweetness was whisked into a police car. Sweetness was gone.

The paddy wagons were full. The Clam House patrons-turned-inmates watched Gladys through the wagons' caged walls. She looked for Toni, but didn't see her. She regretted being mean to Toni. She really was a good makeup woman. The red-faced cop stood in front of Gladys. The Negro cops twisted her arms behind her back so tight she thought they'd snap. She wondered if they'd ever seen her perform, if they'd bought her records, if they'd be gentler if they had. The police had raided The Clam House before. Had these Negro cops taken part? Gladys thought they must have trouble sleeping at night. Her chauffeur lay face down on the ground, head swimming in a rising reservoir of blood. The red-faced cop struck Gladys across the face with his billy club. Blood poured from her mouth like a faucet. He lifted her head by her short-cropped hair and spat in her face. The Negro cops did not loosen their grip. Someone on the sidewalk shouted, "That's Gladys Bentley! You can't do that! That's our Gladys!" The rest of the folks on the sidewalk and the inmates in the paddy wagons took up the shout. "That's Gladys Bentley! You can't do that to Gladys Bentley!"

The cops ignored them.

"There's a special place in hell for nigger men who rape white women," the red-faced cop said. "But until you get there, you got us to deal with."

"I ain't no man," Gladys sputtered. Her lips had ballooned. She could barely get words past them. "I ain't no man. I'm Gla—"

He struck her again. And again. Struck her until her white tuxedo was a canvas of splattered red.

CLEO

I don't want to see you anymore. I'm not feeling it.

The text slammed into Harold's phone. A totally unexpected broadside. He had seen Brett three times in the one week since they met on an app called Trick, and with each date the connection grew deeper. Their first date was at The Windowsill Bar, a decorative travesty with wood paneling, imitation Andy Warhol prints, Christmas lights, Mexican piñatas, and a display case packed with glass phalluses. They started with cocktails and shy, trite talk about the weather before whirling into a grope-fest so ferocious, the doorman warned them to cool it.

Coffee inaugurated dates two and three. Both times they went from espresso to Harold's place and round after round of the most animated sex Harold had had in years. Snuggling filled the time between rounds—fifty-one-year-old Harold locked against the chest of thirty-year-old Brett—as they brainstormed honeymoon locations, each careful to stress the hypothetical nature of such talk.

Harold: "I vote for Rio de Janeiro. I mean, *if* things between us get to that point."

Brett: "Montreal's my first choice. You know, assuming you and I get that far."

By the end of that date, Harold's defenses shattered. One week, three dates. He had run roughshod over infatuation and skipped directly to love. It felt right. Brett made him worthwhile. Worthwhile was a relief from the fear that he wasn't good enough, that there was something wrong with him, something he'd never be able to identify or fix.

As soon as Brett left that night, Harold found an online florist, and sent two bouquets of roses to Brett's house and two to his office.

A fourth date did not materialize.

I'm not feeling it.

Harold did not call Brett. He did not text back. He did not want to hear, *It's not you . . . it's me.* And he was terrified of, *It's not me . . . it's you.*

The next morning he called in sick at his paralegal job, and lay in bed staring at Brett's text. It wasn't a broadside at all. More like a worm that had oozed under the door and lay there, waiting to be discovered, passive-aggressive and cowardly.

Harold grabbed the remote and turned on his favorite guilty-pleasure program: a trash-TV show ablaze with baby-mama drama. Enraged mothers battling to prove that some no-good male was indeed the father. The show was tyrannized by fat Black girls named Shameka with glistening weaves and fat white girls named Becky Rae who lived in trailer parks. Today's episode featured a girl who'd graced the show a few weeks earlier. The scoundrel she'd alleged was her child's father turned out not to be. Now she was accusing a different rascal. The host read the paternity results. "In the case of five-month-old Keisha . . . DeShawn, you are *not* the father!" The audience gasped its shock, its outrage, its delight. The accused man jumped up and down in slaphappy triumph. The defeated mother screamed and ran off the set while a rabid camera crew hurtled after her to capture her humiliated flight for five million shocked, outraged, and delighted daytime viewers.

Harold turned the TV off. He trudged to the bathroom to urinate. He looked at himself in the mirror as he washed his hands. He didn't wear depression well. It amplified his wilting eyes, the bags drooping beneath them. Despite his current melancholy, Harold knew he wasn't ugly, but that few would classify him as handsome. A hookup had once told him he was "pleasant-looking." Harold dried his hands, and thought, *Average*.

He stared into his living room. It was immaculate. When he first moved to Queens and leased this apartment, he'd stood in the empty space for hours, strategizing: furniture placement, picture placement, where on the glossy hardwood floors to station his faux Oriental rugs. He'd mentally assigned his crystal vases, ceramic bowls, and decorative mosaic boxes to specific shelves and accent tables. So when moving day arrived, he'd skipped the interminable arranging and rearranging: his possessions went directly from the moving boxes to their preordained locations which hadn't changed since. He'd always had a flair for decorating. He regretted not pursuing interior design. *Paralegal work is practical*, he—and his parents—had rationalized. A design career hinged on networking, connections, who you knew. When Harold was younger, he hadn't known anybody.

He went to the kitchen. He kept his weed there. It was too early to light up and he didn't care. Today—and perhaps tomorrow—was all about luxuriating in the emerald extravagance of self-pity. He stored his pot in an antique sugar bowl with a *fleur-de-lis* pattern. He always had to remember to hide it when his mother visited from Buffalo. It had slipped his mind last Thanksgiving. Louise Todd needed to sweeten her decaf one morning, found the marijuana, and promptly flushed the $200 stash down the toilet. She spent the balance of her stay pontificating on the perils of narcotics and railed that she had not raised him to be a common druggie.

He was about to light up when he heard a sound, whiny and persistent, outside the door. It sounded like a cat. Harold opened the door.

It *was* a cat. A darling long-haired, gray cat. It looked up at him with pleading in its scared and friendly eyes.

"Hey there, cutie. Where'd you come from?"

Harold stepped toward it, cautiously, afraid it might bolt. It didn't. It let him approach and grazed against his knees when he crouched down to pet it. It purred. Harold looked up and down the hall in search of its owner, but didn't see anyone. The cat had no collar, no identifying information. Harold peeked under the cat. It was a *she*.

"What are you doing in the hall? Did someone in the building put you out?" The cat plunked herself on her back and looked up at him. He rubbed her stomach. She purred some more. "Well, holy shit. What am I gonna do with you?"

The door to the next apartment opened. Annabel stepped into the hall.

"Take her in and keep her," she said. "*That's* what you do with her. Poor thing roamed the halls all night, meowin' and cryin'." Annabel spoke in a snarly Long Island accent, short on *r*'s and *ing*'s and overflowing with corrupted vowels. Listening to her, Harold didn't know whether to laugh or cringe. "Nobody knows who put her out. It's shameful. You need to take her, Gerald."

He'd told her his name more than once. She never remembered. It occurred to him that he was squatting in the hall in his bathrobe and bare feet. He felt inappropriate until he saw Annabel's outfit—one of those thin, frumpy, floral things that old ladies wore. It looked like a nightgown. He was unsure of her age. Sixty? Seventy? She'd banked thirty years in the building to his five.

"I had dogs growing up," Harold said. "I wouldn't know what to do with a cat."

"You feed 'em, you change their litter, and you wait for 'em to pay attention to you." She shook her finger at him. "Someone's gotta take her, Gerald."

Annabel had always been a good neighbor, but her bossiness irked him.

"Why don't *you* take her?" he said. "You like cats."

Annabel dropped her finger. "Well . . . uh . . . sure I do. But I already got one and she's territorial."

Harold stroked the cat's stomach. January penetrated the

building. No radiators or heat in the hall. The chill shrouded the hard floor and numbed Harold's bare feet. How long would the cat survive, freezing as she wandered the building? How long before the super put her outside?

—⫘——⫘——⫘—

I've taken in the abandoned cat that's been roaming the building. If she's yours, please claim her. If she's unclaimed by the end of the week, I'll have to take her to a shelter. — Harold T., Apt. 3K

—⫘——⫘——⫘—

He didn't own a marker to make the sign, so he suspended his self-pitying and went into the world to buy one. While out, he bought a few tins of Grand Kitty Gourmet cat food, some kitty litter, and some cat treats. Harold dithered over the treats, hesitant to spend too much, but she deserved some comfort food. He poured the kitty litter in the aluminum roasting pan his mother had cooked the turkey in last Thanksgiving, then sat on the floor beside her while she dined.

"I'm gonna have to call you something. Hmm. The ancient Egyptians were super fond of cats. And I've always been fond of the Egyptians. How about I call you ... Cleopatra? Yeah. Cleopatra. Good thing you're a girl or I'd have to call you King Tut." Cleopatra jumped in his lap. She purred as he scratched her behind the ears. "Doesn't take much to make you happy, does it? A little scratch. Shelter. Food. That's all you need. Do you know how lucky you are, Cleopatra?" He tickled her whiskers and between her eyes. "Mind if I call you *Cleo*? Shorter names are easier. Just sayin'."

Love and trust shimmered in her alert eyes. Like Brett's eyes their last time in bed. Earnest eyes that gutted Harold's defenses and compelled the swift dispatch of four bouquets of roses.

"Well, Cleo, you and me: we're both members of The Got

Dumped Club. What does that say about us? What's wrong with us? Why doesn't it ever work out? Why is it always more important to us than to the other person?"

Harold cried. Cleo stood on her hind legs in his lap, touching her front paws to his chest to comfort him. She meowed and flicked her tail like a charged wire.

"You're so sweet." He wiped his tears. "But you know this is temporary. I can't afford you. You need food, like, every day, right? And kitty litter, and trips to the vet? Money doesn't grow on trees, Miss Cleo. I could get laid off any time. Can't rely on this economy. You'll have to go to a shelter if no one claims you."

Sweet Cleo at a shelter, subsisting in a cage, waiting to be adopted, perhaps indefinitely. It saddened him. Everybody wanted a kitten, something young and perfect. Nobody wanted something older.

The doorbell buzzed throughout that day. An elderly woman from the second floor gave Harold her old pet carrier. The super brought a proper litter box. "It is not right to make cat go to bathroom in roasting pan," he said in his gravelly Eastern European accent. A first-floor neighbor told him her vet facilitated pet adoptions. Annabel brought three tins of food. Everyone decried the cruelty of abandoning a helpless kitty in a hallway. The flurry sideswiped Harold: except for the super and Annabel, he hadn't met any of these people until today.

The radiator raged. Harold perspired in the boiling apartment. He sniffed an armpit, remembered he'd been too busy lolling in self-pity that morning to shower. At three he stepped into the bathroom. Cleo scratched at the door and meowed to be let in.

"Oh, come on. Can't a guy have some privacy? I'm making myself fresh and pretty."

He removed his clothes, looked in the mirror. He placed his hands on his slightly puffy belly, on his flat, undistinguished chest. For the second time that day he thought, *Average*.

"Maybe that's why Brett wasn't feeling it. He didn't say. They never do."

A gray paw slid under the door.

"Imagine having you to come home to every day, Cleo."

Cleo explored. She invaded closets, hopped onto windowsills, took up residence on the kitchen counter. She propelled herself onto shelves and tables, endangering Harold's strategically arranged bric-à-brac. He held his breath each time she maneuvered her fluid body around a vase and shook his head when she knocked seashells off a shelf.

Her explorations complete, she found him at the computer in his bedroom and invited herself onto his lap. She stared at the screen, inspecting it critically. Harold petted her with one hand, tapped the keyboard with the other, searching out veterinarians.

"Don't get excited. This does *not* mean you're staying. It's research. In case you were to, you know, *hypothetically* stay."

He looked down to find her napping. She seemed at peace. He needed to use the bathroom, but couldn't bear to disturb her—or stop admiring her. She really was gorgeous. Tufts of long, sleek gray fur, such a treat to trail his fingers through. That whip of a tail. And so affectionate. She'd make a good companion. She'd be loyal and consistent. He'd never have to doubt what was in her heart. Never have to worry that she'd change her mind about him. Cleo would never stop loving him.

Imagine having you to come home to every day, Cleo.

Harold's defenses crashed. He clicked the first pet supply site he saw. He bought a carrier, covered litter box, bed, collar, scratching post, and a three-month supply of food and litter. He signed up for pet insurance. Booked an appointment with a vet. Explored a general information cat site: best foods, best exercise, healthiest treats.

"I'll give you wet food once a week. Dry food is better for

your teeth: prevents tartar. Says so right here. Forget table food. What do you think you are, a dog? And you're getting a scratching post, so don't even think about scratching up my couch."

He kissed her.

At seven-thirty they were in the living room, watching TV. A sitcom about an alcoholic lothario who let his loser of a divorced brother and his young son move in with him. Low-brow bathroom humor that assaulted the viewer with a blitzkrieg of fart jokes and big-breast jokes and poop and penis jokes. It was one of Harold's favorite shows.

Cleo idled on his lap. For the first time in years, he didn't dread work the next day. But the thought of leaving her for an entire day was unbearable. He had heard some companies allowed employees to bring pets to work. Something about pets making employees happy, which generated morale, which translated into increased productivity and lower turnover. A pet-induced domino effect. Harold would make his company implement that policy. If it wouldn't, he'd find a job somewhere that would. Maybe an interior design firm. He gave Cleo's head a little scratch. "In the meantime, I have you to come home to every day."

The sitcom ended and another started, this one about a fat delivery driver living in Queens with his thin wife and deranged, socialist father-in-law. Harold thought the delivery driver was kind of hot in his uniform shorts. He had good calves.

The doorbell rang.

"You're popular today, Cleo. That's gotta be yet another neighbor bringing you food. You're the building's top charity case." Harold grinned. "And I'm a hero."

He kissed her, then nudged her off his lap as she meowed in protest. He danced his way through the living room and answered the door.

A young woman stood clutching the sign he'd posted that morning.

"Hi," she said, smiling, apologetic, practically hiding behind the sign. "I'm Jillian. I live on the fifth floor. I think you have my cat."

Harold couldn't talk.

"Sir?" Jillian said. "Harold, right?"

"Yes. Sorry. Come in please."

He ushered her inside. When Cleo saw Jillian, she meowed and hopped off the couch.

"Thank you so much," Jillian said. She hugged Harold. "My fiancé and I ordered takeout last night. She must have slipped out when we were paying the delivery guy. We didn't realize she was gone till now."

Jillian was pretty. Hazel eyes. Streams of polished auburn hair that free-falled over her shoulders and down her back. If he'd been straight, Harold might have been attracted to her.

Jillian picked up Cleo. "Thanks again."

Harold scratched the cat's head. She did not meow. Or look at him. Or seem interested. She was aloof, distant, a cat. Cleo closed her eyes, nestled her head against Jillian's shoulder.

Harold escorted them to the door and they left.

He tried to watch the sitcom. The delivery driver with the good calves was in trouble with his wife and trying to hustle his way out of his latest shenanigans. Harold turned it off. He went to the kitchen and retrieved his pot pipe, still full from the morning. He opened the window, blew the smoke out. The thought of work the next day suffocated him. Maybe he'd call in sick again.

He returned to the living room. Two seashells that Cleo had knocked down still lay on the floor. Paw prints blotched the glass top of his dining-room table. He didn't know she'd hopped up there. He hadn't seen her. The apartment felt empty. Harold smoked more pot. He didn't know Cleo's real name. He'd forgotten to ask Jillian. Would Cleo think about him? Would she care that she spent a nice day with him, that they had liked each other? Harold inhaled on the pipe, deep, deep, and let himself sink. He would definitely call in sick tomorrow.

KISS THE SCARS ON
THE BACK OF MY NECK

1.

You and me had just had our worst fight ever, so I went to the opera.

I did standing room. Always do. Ain't got money for no seat. Even the nosebleed seats is kinda pricey. I stood in the back of the Grand Gallery, two levels up from the orchestra. I dig the fancy name. *Grand Gallery*. Sounds like something rich or big or special, and me right there in it. Or at least standing in back.

I looked around the auditorium, waiting for the show to start. You know how people in old black-and-white movies be all dressed up when they go to the opera or the theater? Guys in tuxes with tails; black bow ties topping off pleated shirts all starched and white with silver buttons; shiny black patent leather shoes. And them silly, boxy top hats that always make me giggle. The women in gowns and pearls and diamonds and fur coats and silky white gloves that stretch all the way up their arms. That's one reason I first wanted to go to the opera, besides the music—the clothes, the glamour, the feeling of stepping into a world that's elegant and exotic.

But that's old movies. Ain't too much glamorous about the

real opera. I mean, you see older men in ties and jackets and some of the women in pantsuits, but that's as fancy as it gets. Mostly it's jeans. Even T-shirts. Even shorts. In old movies, the guys' hair is cut all neat and slicked back and the women's hair is styled like a freakin' architect built that shit and you wonder how it stays up. Well, *I* wonder. You don't like old movies. You never watch them with me.

I was in khakis and a long-sleeve white shirt. No tie, so I fastened the top button to make it look a little better. I took my time ironing my clothes. Used exactly enough starch. I need to look nice when I go to the opera.

I was at the end of the standing-room rail, right on the aisle, flipping through my program. The show was about to start. A guy was standing in the aisle, next to me. Couldn't help noticing him. Three reasons: First, he wasn't wearing no T-shirt and shorts. Dude was styling in a black suit with a red shirt. Second, he was tall—six-four, at least—with door frame-wide shoulders.

Third, he was the only other Black person there.

You usually see two kinda people at the opera. Old. And white. Every now and then there might be someone who looks like us, but usually that's on the stage, 'specially if they're doing *Aida* or *Otello*. And then it's usually white folks painted up to look Black. So it was a big deal seeing a Black dude—'specially dressed like that.

He was looking at his ticket, I guess trying to find his seat. I thought, *I wish I had a seat.* I ain't complaining—if standing room's the only way I can go to the opera, I'm cool with that. But operas is long, yo, I'm talking three, four, five hours. There's this one in German that was six hours. *Six. Hours.* Started at six o'clock and I swear I ain't leave that place till midnight. I stood the whole damn time. So, yeah, I was jealous of that dude. But mostly curious: Black dude in clothes like that *and* sitting in the expensive section? What did he do? How'd he make his money? Did Black folks like you give him shit about liking opera, too?

Another question popped in my head: Would he notice me?

He did. Eyes all blank, like he wasn't sure what he was

seeing, deciding if it was worth seeing. I wanted to talk to him. I sensed he was totally different from me, and not that different, too. I needed to know this man. *Come on, talk to him*, I begged myself. I only had a few seconds 'cause after that he'd be in his seat and the show would start. If I didn't find the guts right then, I never would.

"Enjoy the show," I said. The words came out quiet, but they came. He ain't say nothing back, but his eyes took a tour, traveling from my face all the way down my body, and landed on my shoes. *Shit*, I thought. See, my shirt and khakis looked good, but my shoes was a hot mess. They used to be dark brown, but they was faded to tan and scratched up like I'd scrubbed them with sand. All curled up and raggedy, the heels worn out. Dude shook his head, lips closed tight.

I wished I hadn't said nothing to him.

He went to his seat, stopped and looked at his ticket, and stomped back up the aisle. A couple coming down the aisle got out of his way, like this 6'4", door-frame-shouldered Black man might trample them. He went past me, came back a minute later with an usher. Blonde girl with a ponytail stringing down her back.

"Young lady, I've been a subscriber and high-level contributor for years. I've given $20,000 this year alone. Gifts like mine keep the opera alive—and people like you employed." He didn't shout, but he was heard. His voice slow-burned with authority. Everybody was looking as he held his ticket up like a lawyer showing off evidence in one of them TV court shows. "And this is what you give me," he said. "A seat in a *side* section. Not exactly prime real estate, is it? I cannot express how you've disappointed me this evening."

You'd have thought the usher chose his seat instead of the box office.

"Sir, I apologize," she said, looking left and right and behind her, anywhere but up at this skyscraper of a man. "I'll see if a better seat is available."

"It's too late," he said. "The performance is about to start. But going forward I fully expect you to treat me like the top-shelf contributor I am."

The usher nodded—more like she bowed—and scrambled away. I couldn't help smiling: white girl bowing to a Black man. I wanted him to see me smiling so we could share that. But he went to his terrible seat as the lights went down and the show started.

The opera was *Madame Butterfly*. It's about this Japanese girl who marries an American sailor. Her family's cool with it— till they find out she became a Christian to please her new husband. They cut her off. Won't see her no more, won't talk to her. Nothing. Got to hand it to her: Girlfriend ain't afraid of getting abandoned by the folks she loves.

Melanie, I can tell you how beautiful *Madame Butterfly* is. I can tell you about the voices: how sometimes they purr, sometimes chime, how they hum in my bones. How the orchestra whispers the tender moments, thunders the explosive ones. How the love duet starts with a shiver, then rises like heat.

I can tell you all that. I've tried to. But you don't get it, keep telling me opera's for white folks. Ain't never gonna forget when you said, "Ain't that what gay dudes listen to? Operas and musicals?" But it's more than that: You don't wanna hear 'bout nothing that has to do with what I love. It's always about you. That's why we had our worst fight ever. You know what? Our fight was like opera: an alternate reality that ain't got shit to do with this world, bigger than this world, louder, over the top, full of itself, artificial as hell, but piercing. You hollered out high notes to hurt me. I rumbled low notes to defend myself, convince you, calm you, hold you, beg you. That fight was epic like opera: lasted forever and covered too much ground in a story too fuckin' complicated and bitter to keep track of, so all you can do is listen to the drama. By the time I walked out, looked like you wasn't gonna be my girl no more, I wondered if you ever was, and I knew something I never wanted to admit before: you and me live on different planets, Mel, and there's too much space between us and not enough stars to bridge the gap.

I went to the lobby at intermission. People kept looking at

me. No. They was looking at my hot-mess shoes. Eyes whizzing right to them. They ain't see *me*. Now, there was white dudes with untucked shirts and wrinkled pants; white chicks who hadn't been to a beauty shop in a hundred years and had the split ends to prove it. But my shoes made them shake their heads. I saw a Black couple, only ones besides me and that fancy dude going off 'bout his seat. Wasn't much older than me, him in a blue suit, her in a cream-colored dress, super-high heels, and a weave Beyoncé would have strangled her for. The guy turned his nose up and away so fast, I was surprised he ain't get whiplash, but the chick nodded and smiled. I nodded back. When the guy saw that, he put his hand on the small of her back and scooted her into the auditorium. She shot him a mean look, and looked over her shoulder at me and mouthed, *I'm sorry.*

Something about how she looked at her boyfriend, something about that over-the-shoulder apology, reminded me of you, Mel. A softer you. A kinder time when you defended me from dudes like that chick's boyfriend. I want that time back. I want that softer you.

Everybody at intermission was talking and drinking in clique-y groups. Reminded me of the playground at school. You remember—the cool kids in their own group, the nerdy kids in theirs, the outcasts on the sidelines. I ain't have money for a drink and nobody to talk to, so I was the outcast. I'd already read every page of my program, but I read it again and tuned everything and everybody out. That's why the voice surprised me.

"Call it a *performance*, not a *show*."

I looked up and saw a chest in front me wearing a red satin-y shirt. Well, almost wearing. It was unbuttoned so far down, I mostly saw skin. I looked up, higher, into the face of the fancy suit guy, holding two tall glasses of champagne in his dark hands, the nails buffed shiny.

"You call a theater production or a concert or a supper club act a show," he said. "Call an opera a show and you'll be branded an amateur. And the last thing you want to be at the opera is an amateur."

He held one of the glasses out to me. I wasn't sure I should take it.

"Oh, come now. It's a gift," he said, but I still ain't take it. "You're hurting my feelings."

"Man, you don't even know me."

He swirled the champagne around his glass. "My dear, that can be easily rectified."

Ain't never been called that by no man before. *My dear.* It eased off his tongue. Smooth. Sophisticated. His lips was closed, the corners ticked up in a little smile. He looked me in the eyes. He didn't blink.

My dear.

I took the champagne. "Thank you." I think I stuttered it. My neck got stiff from looking up at him. My ass is 5'7". He made me feel like a freakin' dwarf.

"Paul Crane."

Took me a minute to realize he was introducing hisself.

"Cedric Curtis," I said.

He touched his glass against mine, held it there a few seconds. "Lovely to meet you. Cedric Curtis."

Lovely to meet you. Cedric Curtis. Like words to this guy were sugar or pretty flowers or a pretty song. Something sweet to be shared. And he was sharing it with *me?* It was mad awkward for a minute. I ain't know what to say. I kept looking this way and that, anywhere but at that ticked-up smile.

"I brought you this champagne and you've barely drunk any."

Sounded like he was criticizing, so I took a sip. Dude was watching me. I needed to say something, anything.

"Did you really give the opera $20,000?"

"Do you doubt the veracity of what I told that usher?"

He cocked his head sideways on *veracity*. Probably thought I ain't know what it meant. Probably thought I was stupid. "Yeah, I did doubt the veracity of what you said. I figured you was lying to get a better seat."

He did blink now. I pounced again before he could recover. "You was nasty to that girl. Wasn't her fault you got a bad seat."

Now he looked like something had came at him out of nowhere, blindsided him, and something told me Paul Crane wasn't used to getting blindsided.

I went in for the kill. "You should be ashamed of yourself. Pick on someone your own size."

I felt like a champ juiced up after a knockout punch. But Paul's close-lipped, ticked-up smile came back. He'd been bending at the shoulders to get his face closer to mine, but now he straightened up to his real height. He looked down at me. "It would be savagely unfair to pick on someone *your* size."

I take things personal. Daddy used to get on me about that, said, "Baby, to survive in this world you better grow skin like a rhinoceros. You don't, and folks'll tear you up and spit on the pieces." I've tried hard to do like he said, but mean words eat through my thin skin. But when Paul said that shit 'bout my size, I damn near laughed. 'Cause inside this big man in a fancy suit was a petty little boy who got his ass called out by a kid from the hood in bad shoes. What's fucked up is the man didn't even know it about hisself. I guess when you look in the mirror every day, you get blind to shit that everybody else sees right away.

He brushed something off my right shoulder. "I assure you . . . ," the left shoulder, " . . . that I did contribute $20,000 . . . ," he straightened my collar, took longer than he needed to, " . . . and that it was neither the sole, nor by any means the largest contribution I've made to this venerable institution. It was merely the most recent."

He put his champagne glass against my cheek. The glass was wet. It was like he was kissing me. I kinda liked it. Well. More than kinda.

Something I ain't never told you, Melanie: I mess around with dudes.

Yeah, that's right. *Mess around*, as in have sex, suck a dick, then spread my ass and let it inside me. I meet them on the train, or on the street, or in grocery stores. Sometimes they ask me to go home with them, and I do. Or I'll lock eyes with one, and he'll cock his head toward a restroom or a parked car or a empty

128

part of a subway platform, and I'll follow. I like girls more, I like *you* more, but I like dudes, too. Giving in to a man is different from giving in to a woman. Dudes don't take each other too serious, so there ain't as much to lose. Never told you 'cause I didn't think you'd get it. So much about me you don't get. But in your mind the opera thing probably makes sense now.

Whatever. I been with enough dudes to know what Paul Crane wanted. But did *I* want it?

An usher came through, ringing a bell. Intermission was over.

"Thanks very much for the champagne," I said. "Well. Nice meeting you."

It was mad awkward again. I wanted to get away from Paul Crane. And I wanted him to keep me there, try again to eat through my thin skin.

"A friend of mine was supposed to accompany me this evening," Paul said. "Something came up at the last minute and he couldn't make it. So I have an unoccupied seat right next to mine. Join me."

Wasn't sure I should. And I was relieved he asked.

You'd think opera seats would be the most comfortable seats in the world. They ain't. Stiff cushions. No leg room. Paul's long legs was all scrunched in. The lights was going down, he turned in his seat, put his mouth right on my ear.

"By the way, I'm an artist. A painter. World-renowned, I might add."

He faced front again. I felt a cool draught where his mouth had been.

The *performance* started. I waited for Paul's hand on my thigh, but he kept his hands to hisself.

I was glad. I was disappointed.

2.

When you see him at the standing room rail, your first thought is not *God, he's cute*, though his lineless boy-face transfixes you.

Nor is your first thought that he needs to get his shoes someplace other than some tragic last-chance bin at the Salvation Army. And though this is that rare occasion on which you see a young Black man at the opera, that is also not your debut thought.

You certainly do think all of these things, but your first thought, or rather, your first *sense*, is his fear, so thick it rolls off him. And loneliness, too, or, more specifically, more poignantly, his alone-ness. It hovers about him like an aura. He glows with solitude. You're drawn to his light.

Your seat is fine. You don't mind side sections. You're not a snooty, entitled opera patron, although you have friends who are. Here's what happens: You see him, become instantly besotted, go to your seat, and can't bear not having another look. You can turn around easily enough, but what if he isn't looking back? You won't risk him not noticing you. So you march back up the aisle and throw a hissy fit that likely ruins that poor usher's entire evening. Unfortunate, but it's the only way. Your evening is more important than hers.

It's aggressive, bringing him the champagne, as is chastising him for referring to the opera as a *show* (but s*how* is gauche and he needs to know it). Far more aggressive is inviting him to sit with you for the second act. No one cancelled on you. Your companions do not cancel on you. You encourage the bored, texting gentleman in the adjacent seat not to return after intermission. $300 cash sweetens the suggestion. The curtain rises and you become aggressive with yourself and keep your hands off the boy by exerting an exceptional force of will.

When the performance ends, the two of you head toward the cars and taxis lined up on the street. A driver steps out of a limo and opens the door for you. There it is again: that fear. Cedric thinks you're going to ask him to come home with you. You sense he both does and does not want to. It isn't the first time this evening that dual and dueling vibes have radiated off this boy. It's moot, though, because you have no such intention. Not for tonight, that is. Cedric Curtis is a delight to be savored, not hastily devoured like the slutty boys you're used to from the apps.

You hand him your card—*If you ever want to talk*—then slip into the limo and you're gone.

You know he won't reach out right away. Not tonight or tomorrow or the next day, and perhaps not the following week. But he will. Because you touched something in him. A vulnerable spot. A void that emits a quiet, barefaced yearning, one that needs filling, bolstering. He'll come to you for that. He has no one else to go to. You don't know how you know that, but you do.

Yes, you're confident he'll reach out, even though he's already seen that you're a challenge (most people dispense with the euphemism and just say *difficult*). You enjoyed that little sparring match at intermission. Part of it was cutting him down to size, so to speak, but the greater enjoyment was that he sparred with you at all. He relished going up against you. You saw it in the assertive crane of his neck as he looked up into your face and told you off, in his hurling that double whammy, accusing you of falsehoods and rudeness. You weren't speechless because he bested you, but because you were so delighted that he dared to.

So. You wait. In the meantime you go about your business. Ruthless patience is one of your better qualities.

You weren't exaggerating when you said you're a world-renowned painter. With works exhibited in galleries and museums and private collections across the globe, anyone remotely associated with the art world knows Paul Crane. So you do what you always do: paint, work on your commissions, email gallery owners and your agents and current and prospective clients. You drop in at cocktail parties with movie stars and bestselling writers in Tribeca lofts, and your clothes, connections, and bribes win you entrée to swank clubs in Soho. No waiting in line for you. Ever. You attend Broadway premieres, charity events, political fundraisers where you make a point of getting photographed with mayors, governors, and senators of both parties.

And you think about Cedric Curtis.

He's pleasant to think about. That short, slim body. Not much muscle on it, you suspect, unlike your ripped and sculpted rent boys, and a complete contrast with your own grandly muscular body that, at forty-eight, still turns heads. Cedric's body is pretty and small enough to fit in your arms, snug as a puzzle piece. The thought intrigues you. In your arms, would that glow of solitude ebb, or would it spread to you, encasing both of you in its ember? That thought intrigues you, too.

But now it's been three weeks, and no word. You try not to think about him but before you know it, you've got an obsession on your hands. The insidious thing sneaks up on you and claws your ruthless patience. To salve the wound you prowl your sex apps—you're particularly fond of the one called Trick—and trap every half-interested man who ambles across your radar. You regret not taking Cedric home that night. But at the precise moment that regret threatens to rupture into full-blown misery, a text arrives.

hey its cedric from the opera wanna get together

The shortage of punctuation makes it unclear whether *get together* is a request or a declaration. That's neither here nor there because a tsunami of relief bludgeons you.

Since he's forced you to wait three weeks, you don't text right back. That evening you hook up with a musclebound, intellectually challenged specimen on Trick. After he departs, you fall into a candied sleep that leaves you more refreshed than you've been in weeks. Three to be exact.

You text Cedric in the morning.

Meet me at Imperial Coffee, tomorrow at 1pm. Look up the address.

He replies right away.

how about today

Meeting today requires cancelling an appointment with a surly Belgian opera baritone who's recently exploded to stardom.

He's establishing his home base in New York, purchasing an apartment in the West Village. He's commissioned you to create a piece for the foyer. He won't take kindly to your cancelling, but the contract is signed so he can go fuck himself.

You arrive first. You assume Cedric won't be on time (why do you assume that?), but he walks in at the appointed hour. He stays near the entrance, hands in his pockets, that glow of fear and solitude beaming. He's wearing a hoodie, sneakers, tight jeans that magnify and glorify his skinniness. Something regarding his appearance bothers you. You're relieved he doesn't have a doo-rag on his head or loose pants hanging beneath his waist and his backside bulging out. But that hoodie. It causes him to stand out in this Upper East Side coffee shop in a way that a similarly attired young white man would not.

You wave him over. He comes, slowly, and sits, head hunched down. His eyes do not meet yours or even look for them. That hurts. You did not expect that.

"It's lovely to see you," you say. He nods, but says nothing. "Get your coffee."

"That's OK. I ain't thirsty."

You cringe. Growing up, you were strictly trained in the art of correct English. Your mother was ruthless: Justine Ward Crane didn't play when it came to grammar. She once punished you when an *ain't* inadvertently slipped out of your nine-year-old mouth. She blamed *Popeye*, convinced your favorite cartoon character's atrocious English was the negative influence that instigated your grammatical crime. You've inherited her love for and insistence on correct English, so Cedric Curtis is already proving a challenge.

"This is the second time you've tried to make me drink alone," you say.

You mean that to be funny, but he takes it seriously. He keeps his head and eyes down. "I ... I ain't got no money," he murmurs. "If you could get me some coffee, I'd appreciate that, Paul."

That tsunami from yesterday makes a reprise, except this time it's heartbreak that bludgeons you. You know what it's like

133

to be broke. When you were growing up, Justine sometimes worked multiple jobs to support you and your half-brother William, and still the household suffered from a dearth of money. A dearth deep enough to create a pall of anxiety. You've had hordes of young men ask for a hell of a lot more than coffee, and as if they were entitled. But Cedric has the decency to be embarrassed. His humility conquers you.

You reach across the table and touch his shoulder. "How do you like it?"

"A little milk and sugar. Thank you." It's a whisper, but he lifts his eyes to you for the first time since he arrived, and this eases your hurt.

"Why did you want to meet?" you ask after you've brought his coffee.

"Needed to see you."

Needed, not *wanted*. You note the distinction.

"What's wrong, my dear? What's happened?"

"Someone I really love won't talk to me. We had a bad fight."

He holds it back, but a hurricane of tears is amassing in his eyes. Brown eyes, very pretty, and trained on you as if pleading.

"Not the first bad fight, I take it," you say. Cedric nods with the weary air of a young man in possession of an old soul. "When?"

"Few weeks ago. Same night as the opera. I keep calling, texting. Nothing."

In the silence that follows, you wrestle with how far to inquire into this bad fight. You're terrified of overstepping. The consequence could be another three weeks of obsession and no word from him. But he comes to your rescue.

"Mel sees other guys. It's killing me."

No hyperbole here—the hurricane is on the cusp of landfall—but you suppress a giggle at his archaic notion of monogamy, one to which you've never subscribed. Monogamy is an asinine thing to aspire to: human beings are not designed for it. You're irritated that he took three weeks to reach out only to cry over some other man; irritated that he has a boyfriend at all, though details like boyfriends, partners, and spouses can generally be worked around.

After pausing a respectful amount of time, you say, "I'm glad you reached out."

Another silence while he looks at you, contemplates you, probably aching to trust you and assessing whether it's safe. But you wonder if anyone with a halo of solitude is capable of trust, whether true solitude is rooted so deep that trust can never reach it. Will Cedric Curtis let you in? If so, how far?

Cedric's contemplation segues to inspection as he takes in the breadth of your shoulders, the biceps testing the limits of your short sleeves, your forty-eight-year-old face that's nearly as lineless as his. Moments pass before he says, "Glad I reached out, too."

You settle in, learn one another's basics. Cedric Curtis is twenty-four; born and raised in the Bronx; lives with a roommate in Jackson Heights, Queens; works at a bodega, delivering or cashiering or sweeping or some such; was enrolled in community college for a couple of semesters before dropping out—you scold him for that—but he's interested in web design, HTML, Photoshop; got his hands on an ancient laptop with bootleg software that allows him to play web designer, but has made no substantive moves toward pursuing an education in that field.

"You won't become a web designer by futzing around on an old computer," you say. "You have to get the training."

"Maybe one day."

You collapse against the cushioned back of your chair. "Good god." You shake your head. "Millennials. You think the world is waiting for you to show up, clamoring for you to grace it with your amazing presence, that it'll hand you a trophy when you finally do. I have news for you, my dear: It won't."

Cedric's lips twitch. He rubs the back of his neck. The twitching lips settle into a grimace and the boy-face transforms to a concrete mask as his narrowed eyes take aim at you. He rubs his neck again. You hold your breath. You're afraid he'll walk out. Once it's evident he won't, you exhale a triumphant breath and allow yourself to revel. Getting under his skin was as effortless as it was satisfying. You think back to the sparring match at the opera: All about besting each other. Is that what's shaping up here? A relationship whose fabric is woven with contention? The fibers taut with it, dependent on it? Is this the natural state of things between you and Cedric Curtis?

"The night we met—I assume it was your first time at the opera," you say. "What did you think?"

Cedric's narrowed eyes burn. The concrete mask melts, or rather, oozes, into a shrewd smile. "Why you assume it was my first time?" He lengthens *assume*, endows the vowel with extra weight. If his question were set to music, *assume* would be a high note. And if this were chess, his move would be checkmate.

Damn.

He got you, snagged you in a trap of your own making. Because in asking that question about the opera, you made the same assumption a white person might.

You've patronized the opera for decades, contributed hundreds of thousands of dollars, never missed a season. Yet you can't count the times the white person in the next seat has said, *You must be new to opera.* Or chatting at intermission: *I'm glad you're enjoying it. Opera's more challenging than R&B. Or jazz, even.* You're doing the same thing to this young man. You've wronged him. You're embarrassed. You should apologize, but the words *I'm sorry* do not reside in your vocabulary. Instead you sit forward, make your eyes burn like his. "Given your shoes that night, I reasonably *assumed* it was your first time. Experienced operagoers know better."

He picks up his coffee, sets it down. The cup makes a staccato clinking against the table because Cedric's hand is trembling. He rubs the back of his neck again and hardens his lips into a tight, unyielding line. He might really walk out this time.

Do something. Keep him here.

"How long have you been going to the opera?" you ask.

"I don't know."

"What's your favorite?"

You're not sure he'll answer. At last he says, "*La Bohème.*"

"That's a great one," you say, although *Bohème* is rather too standard for your taste. Saying one's favorite opera is *La Bohème* or *Carmen* or *La Traviata* is like saying one's favorite color is blue. Every common person in the world likes blue. *Your* favorite operas are: *Pelléas and Mélisande, Die Entführung aus dem Serail, Samson et Dalila, Tannhäuser,* and *Les Pêcheurs des Perles,* which is also Justine's favorite. No plain old blue there. More like cerulean. Or lapis. Glinting turquoise. But you tell Cedric, "*Bohème's* my favorite, too." His burning eyes cool. You seize on that. "You and Mel: Are you officially boyfriends or just dating?"

"Mel's short for Melanie. She's officially my girlfriend."

You are shocked. It must be obvious because a smirk gloats on Cedric's lips. His body loosens and he slides down in his chair. When he picks up his coffee again, his hand is surgeon-steady. He drains the cup, plunks it back on the table. You're furious, but you admire him: The boy knows how to land a hit. More important, he knows not to overdo it, to simply sit back after decisively winning a round.

You want a sip of coffee, but it would be *your* hand trembling this time, and you're not about to let him see that. "Tell me about Melanie."

"We fight a lot."

"You said that already, dear."

He picks up his coffee cup, but it's empty. You pluck a credit card from your wallet and flick it—intentionally—so that it lands on the floor, a couple of feet from him.

"Pick it up. Get a refill," you say. "And then you're going to tell me why you and Melanie fight a lot."

He isn't quick to obey. He remains seated so long, you wonder if he's going to leave your credit card on the floor. Already more than one patron—espressos and lattes and smartphones in hand—has taken inquisitive note of the card as they stepped around it. It's an eternity before Cedric picks it up and goes to the barista.

You liked telling him what to do. It's made your dick hard.

He must have liked it, too, because when he comes back, you don't have to prompt him. He divulges that he's been seeing this Melanie/Mel girl a few years, that they fight because they see the world differently.

You plant your elbows on the table and lean forward as if you mean to leap across it. "You've got to do far better than that, my dear. Do you think your situation is unique from millions of other couples?" You mimic him in a munchkin voice. "*Me and Mel fight because we see the world differently.* That's the feeblest excuse I've heard all week."

Paul, Paul, Paul.

You can't resist going too far and panicking afterward that the boy will bolt. Act first, manage the damage later. You've done it all your life. You get off on risk, although it sometimes bites you, and extracting its teeth can prove troublesome. But—once again—you've lucked out because Cedric shakes his head and smiles, which gives you the confidence to lift your coffee cup without fear of a trembling hand.

You take a luxurious sip of cappuccino. "I wonder what you're not telling me. What's the real reason you and Melanie fight?" Your turn to make music: you sing *real* like it's the lowest, most grumbling note in an opera villain's aria. "Maybe you don't truly want to be with Melanie."

"Who you think I truly wanna be with? You?"

"Perhaps."

Cedric grunts. "You probably twice my age."

"And a man."

"Yeah. You probably that, too."

A quick, curt quiet before you and Cedric bombard Imperial Coffee with rockets of laughter. The young staff is amused, but a tableful of prim, middle-aged customers glares; a businesswoman in pantsuit and white sneakers looks up from her laptop. She shakes her head at you two Black men cutting up in this highfalutin Upper East Side coffee shop. And you wonder if this rocketing laughter, this soothing of defenses following a blaze of tension, are also woven through this relationship, alongside the contention. Will this be the pattern? Provoke. Escalate. Fight. Ease down.

Then what?

The laughter recedes, the avalanche of seriousness tumbles back down.

"I guess I'm bi," Cedric says, "but I like women more."

"You're only a boy. You need a man to teach you what you like."

You extend a hand across the table and grasp his. He maneuvers it out of your grip, folds his arms across his chest, adjusts his body so that it's angled away from you, which speaks more loudly than if he walked out. Time to implement drastic measures. It takes one split-second to concoct a plan.

"I have to go," you say. You rise, place a hand on his shoulder. There's something on the back of his neck. Several somethings. Lines. Some short, others longer. Some of them raised and puckered, embossing the skin. Scars. A tangle of them, criss-crossing Cedric's neck, like thin, brushstroked lines on an abstract painting. Your thumb grazes the scars. The grazing coaxes you to a reverie. You lose yourself in the intimacy of touching this lovely young man. You're alarmed at the violence that has been inflicted on him, leaving these scars as residue. *Who did this to you? Why did you let them?* You grow so protective so rapidly, it overwhelms you.

I won't let anyone do this to you again.

You come back to yourself, remember your plan. You tell him goodbye and fling yourself toward the exit.

Countdown time:

Five.

Four.

Three.

T—

"Paul!"

Cedric's coming toward you, as you hoped (knew) he would. Your credit card is in his hand, as you knew (hoped) it would be.

"Keep it," you say. "Give it to me next time."

139

3.

A freakin' tug of war, Mel.

That's what it was like dealing with Paul Crane. Sometimes pulling, sometimes getting pulled. Back and forth, back and forth. Teeth gritting and grinding down to the root. Knowing it's a game, but we got rope burns on our hands. Back and forth. Sometimes he was winning, sometimes I was. But in the end we ain't do nothing but pull at each other. And enjoy the hell out of it, rope burns and all.

He told me he was a famous painter first night we met, but I ain't Google him till after that coffee. He wasn't lying: dude got paintings all over the damn world. New York. L.A. London. Singapore. Berlin. Amsterdam. Beijing. Found his website. Bio said he was mentored by this white artist named Myron Hillhouse who got famous painting Black versions of classical and historical white guys. Paul Crane painted Black versions of white icons, too—but his M.O. was women. Queen Elizabeth I. Betsy Ross. Juliet. Eleanor Roosevelt.

Famous artist. Interested in me.

Wasn't sure what to do with that. Wasn't sure I deserved it. Wasn't sure I wanted it.

'Specially since he's a dick.

Tug. Of. War.

Paul Crane brought out the worst in me. He insulted me, made me feel like I wasn't good enough or smart enough. But he brought out the best, too. Made this shy boy stand up for hisself. Made me give as good as I got. Made me know that I could. I'm grateful for that. I ain't always stood up for myself. So many times I let people shit on me. That's how I got these scars on my neck. But you know better than anybody how I got these scars.

Yeah. Paul Crane. Worst and best. If I had money, I'd bet I brought out the worst and best in him, too.

Ain't got money. Got his credit card.

Give it to me next time.

When's next time, Mr. Famous Artist?

Wonder if he gonna reach out. I made him wait three weeks—he gonna make me wait, too? Maybe I'll go to the opera to fill the time. Use his credit card to buy me a seat in the Grand Gallery. *La Bohème.* My fave and his. When he told me that, made me feel like we . . . I don't know. Like we bonded or something.

When he asked me how long I been going to the opera, I said I didn't know.

I lied.

Sophomore year of high school, they took us on a field trip to the opera. Nobody wanted to go. Kids was mad 'cause they was making us. I was mad, too. I ain't want to hear no classical bullshit. The more militant kids marched to the principal's office, protesting. "Niggers ain't supposed to go no opera!" they shouted. "It ain't natural. It's white." Some of them had signs. They made us go anyway.

On the bus ride, Mr. Hastings, the music teacher, said, "Ladies and gentlemen, a night at the opera isn't the end of life as you know it." He wore a bow tie and penny loafers. Somebody said, "Black faggot," under their breath but loud enough to hear. Mr. Hastings pretended he didn't. I think Mr. Hastings did lots of pretending.

They stuck us in this section called the Presenters' Circle, halfway between the ground floor and the nosebleed. Auditorium was mad large, like a stadium, but prettier. Plush red carpet and red velvet seats and dark wood railings. Stage curtain made of gold cloth that shimmered. A dozen baby crystal chandeliers hanging from the ceiling, surrounding a granddaddy chandelier, sparks of light firing through them crystals. I was freakin' dazzled, but I tried not to be. The musicians was warming up. People was taking their seats. I thumbed through my program. In class, Mr. Hastings had said *La Bohème* was about this poor-as-shit poet who falls in love with a girl who dies of TB at the end. "Yeah," the kid in the next desk had said. "That's what I want to see—some sick bitch die."

The chandeliers drifted up into the ceiling. Folks got quiet.

The auditorium got dark. My heart beat fast. I ain't expect that. The gold curtain rose. The first scene was a bunch of men living together in a attic in Paris. "Must be fags," kid next to me said out loud. "No wonder Hastings loves this boring mess." People shushed him.

The opera wasn't boring. It wasn't no mess.

It was supernatural. From some other world. Some other dimension. Some weird, bright place between earth and heaven. It didn't belong here, but it was here anyway. I loved it, and I understood why people didn't. It was too different. People hate different. Different makes folks nervous. It's a page they can't read 'cause the words is alien. Different fucks with their comfort zone, makes them suspicious. People take different personal, like it's a insult to them. They want to think something's wrong with different, but really they're scared there's something wrong with themselves.

I sat there. I listened. Half my classmates was texting. The other half was asleep. But I was more awake than I'd ever been. I didn't know voices could sound like that, could climb so high and swoop so low. That they could blaze like that. Roar like that. The big, loud moments was a volcano. The quiet ones was poems. The voices hypnotized me. I ain't care 'bout the story—guy named Rodolfo, chick named Mimi, they fall in love, she moves into the attic, he's always jealous, she pushes back, they fight, break up, she gets sick, she dies, whatever. At one point I closed my eyes and just soaked up the music. Soaked *in* the music. Dunked myself in that shit. Fuckin' drowned in it. Moon and sun and stars in my ears. A gold mine in my ears. Pearls, diamonds. Sparks. Shadows. Rage. Rainbows. Velvet. Hurricanes.

Next day I went to the opera's website, found out standing room tickets was pretty cheap. Week after, I got me a job after school and started going to the opera.

Couldn't help loving it.

Couldn't help feeling I'd been seduced by something that I ain't have no business being seduced by.

Couldn't help loving it anyway.

4.

Lacy lingerie that shows off the best of you. Emerald necklace—your birthstone, your favorite. Dinner at some fancy restaurant where the waiters wear white gloves and tuxes and the maître d' guy pulls your chair out for you. A weekend at a bed and breakfast in some dope town on a beach. All for you, Mel. And stuff for me, too: new sneakers, new phone, good computer with legit software.

Oh yeah, some dress shoes for the opera. Hard-soled and shiny.

Paul Crane's credit card was throbbing in my wallet. I could have got all that stuff and more, but I settled for a dozen red roses. For you. Couldn't wait to give them to you. Took the F train to Park Slope, got off at Fourth Ave., bought the roses at the bodega where the cashier always flirting with me *and* trying to set me up with her daughter, and headed toward your place. Head up, chest puffed out, proud to bring something pretty to my pretty Mel. Had my earbuds in, listening to *The Elixir of Love*. Yes, Mel, an opera. Cute one too. 'Bout this peasant guy in love with a rich girl who don't notice him most times, and treats him like crap when she do. Peasant guy drinks a love potion that's supposed to make the girl fall in love with him, but it ain't nothing but wine, so only thing happens is he gets drunk off his peasant ass.

I looked at the roses and thought, *Maybe these'll be my love potion.*

Missed you much, girl. Hadn't talked in three weeks. Hurt deep you wouldn't answer the phone, return my texts. Felt like you was ghosting me. Hoped showing up at your door with a armful of roses would make everything good. Hoped you was missing me as hard as I was missing you, that it was pride kept you from picking up the phone and not that you ain't love me.

Melanie.

We was little kids together, girl. All through school. Wasn't for you, I wouldn't have had no friends. First day of kindergarten, all the boys had sat at one table, all the girls at another. And there was me, trembling in a corner, scared to approach both. Scared of the boys who was already fondling *nigger* like a new toy, and scared of the girls 'cause they was all dresses and ribbons and long hair and dolls and I wasn't supposed to like all that but did. Miss Ellis kept saying, "Cedric, come sit," and I stayed trembling in that corner, so she sucked her teeth and said, "Lord have mercy. These shy children gonna be the death of me," and went on leading the kids through the alphabet. She was at *M* when you got up and took my hand. "Sit over here," you said, and dragged me to a seat next to you at the girls' table. After that, I always had a table to sit at and at least one friend.

I thought you was pretty. And every time you defended me or told off some boy who was teasing me or protected me from somebody pushing me around, you got prettier. You still so pretty, Mel, but I don't know what happened to you. Yeah, I do: You figured out how pretty you was. Figured out how to use that.

I tried not to think 'bout that. I propped a big smile on my lips, put a bop in my step, and turned onto your street. And I saw it: a black Jag, parked in front of your building. It stood out from the Dodges and Toyotas and Chevies like a big ol' gold sword among rusty knives.

Leland's car.

My hand shook as I dug your housekeys out my pocket. You ain't know I had them. A few months back, I took your keys when you was sleeping, got them copied. This was why.

I ran up to the second floor and let myself in your apartment. Leland was sitting on the couch in his boxers and his chalky white skin and man-breasts that drooped. I've done it with white dudes with nipples all pink and plump. But his was chalky as the rest of him. Flat, too. His hair was thin, mostly blond with flares of gray threading through it. Big ol' bald spot in the middle of his head, some strings of hair combed over it and glued in place with gel. The bags under his eyes was droopy as his breasts. He wore gold rings on, like, six fingers, gold so bright they looked stupid on someone so pale.

Leland looked up. "You again. The opera boy."

A money clip with a fat lump of bills sat on the coffee table. Leland nabbed it, set it behind him.

Already knew the answer, but I asked, "Why are you here?" I wanted to shout, but it came out like a whimper. *The Price Is Right* was on the TV. Some dude had spun the big wheel and won ten thousand dollars and a spot in the showcase. The audience was going mad crazy. Leland's clothes was next to him on the couch, but he ain't reach for them like he reached for that money clip. I heard the shower going in the bathroom. Had you already done it with him and you was cleaning up? Or was you getting ready for him?

The back of my neck itched bad. I wanted to rub it, but I wouldn't let myself. My hands shook. The roses shook with them.

"Melanie and me are . . ." He crinkled his forehead, looked off into space, like he was looking for the right word. He found it: " . . . busy."

Inside, in the pit of me, I felt a tremor. Light, but rumbling.

Leland latched his fingers together, popped his knuckles. The sound was like nuts cracking open. "Come back later."

Another tremor. From that same pit, but climbing up, toward my throat. My throat closed. I had to breathe deep so I could croak out the words. "Leave Mel alone. Why don't you leave her alone?"

Leland shrugged, lifted his hands, palms up. "I don't call her. She calls me."

"She's *my* girl."

"Treat her like she is, junior, and she won't need to call me. But when she calls, I *will* come. Pun intended. You know what a pun is, junior?"

He laughed like his joke was the funniest thing ever. He peeled a hundred-dollar bill off his money clip. That shit was so crisp, I thought it might break. I could almost smell the green ink. "Here. Take this. Go buy yourself something. Be a good

145

junior. I'll tell Mel to call you."

He held the money out to me. The tremor inside me spiked into a full-on earthquake. I whipped him across the face with the roses and marched into the bathroom and yanked back the shower curtain so hard, the plastic tore, the hooks went flying. There you were. First time I'd seen you in weeks. You pressed your hands over your tits. Like I ain't seen them before. Like I ain't have no right to.

"What's he doing here?" I shouted. "You broke again? Landlady's nagging about the rent? Or did he promise to take you to some fancy place for dinner? Or shopping? You been talking about getting away, maybe you sweet-talked him into taking you on vacation. Sweep you off to some cozy island where you can get away from it all. Get away from *me*."

You screamed at me to get out, we'll talk about it later, call me tomorrow, but go, Cedric, get out of here. Your eyes jerked to something behind me. I swiveled around. Leland was standing in the bathroom door. He'd put on his pants, but not his shirt or shoes. Now that he was upright, he ain't look so old and frail. Kinda flabby, but squat and muscular. The man-breasts made him barrel-chested, powerful. Motherfucker grabbed me by the collar, jammed me in a headlock, and hauled me to the living room so fast, I barely knew what the fuck happened. He barked at you to get out here, open the front door, come on, hurry up. You ran out wrapped in a towel, shower water sloshing off you. Leland wrestled me out of the apartment, kicked me down the stairs like you'd kick in a door. I crash-landed in the lobby. Heads poked out of apartments, people gathered on the stairs to watch me, clumped and squirming. Leland came down—still shirtless—with what was left of the roses and flung them on top of me. I heard the door slam after he went back up, but I ain't hear you scream at him. I ain't hear you give him hell for what he did. I listened, listened hard. But I ain't heard nothing.

5.

The *Tannhäuser* overture plays on the sound system. You're in your studio, applying the final brushstrokes to your latest piece. A commission for a new client: a floor to ceiling, wall to wall painting of Joan of Arc. The client is an entrepreneur, millionaire, and sometime talk radio commentator. She's also politically ultraconservative, which has cut a rift in several of your relationships. People are saying that accepting her money makes you part of the problem; that she's using you—a Black artist—to give herself cover from the charges of racism that perpetually bedevil her. They're calling you a collaborator, an Uncle Tom. Some friends have urged you to drop the commission. Some have begged. Others have demanded: Drop it or the friendship is over. You despise threats, so those demanding individuals now fall under the category of *former friends*.

The overture mounts in a strapping wave of melody. Brilliant opera. *Tannhäuser* is about consummate surrender to art and pleasure, to beauty and debauchery. Never mind that it also concerns the alleged spiritual consequences of that surrender. It's one of your favorite operas. Just as Joan of Arc is one of your favorite historical figures. You've yearned to paint her, but not in the regal, saintly way she's traditionally been depicted, clad in golden armor astride a majestic battle horse, sinless eyes lifted to heaven as she marshals French troops against the English. Your Joan is more ferocious than saintly. Armor dulled to a battle-scarred tarnish, she's on the ground amidst a conflagration of mayhem—wild, sword-wielding French and English soldiers; whinnying horses rearing tall on hind legs; flags and tents and woods roaring with flames. Joan's ragged horse watches as she raises her sword high in clenched hands to ram it through the heart of a fallen, terrified English soldier. Historical purists will excoriate you because the real Joan never killed anyone—supposedly—and because your Joan is Black, as are the heroines in all your paintings.

Reverse cultural appropriation.

Political correctness on steroids.

Callous Africanizing of a beloved European icon.

What if MLK were depicted as Caucasian? Would that be acceptable?

Critics regurgitate the same litany of grievances each time you unveil a new painting. You withstand the indignant social media blowback, the hate mail, the right-wing media's gleeful evisceration. It's all fine. It makes you more famous, and fame attracts commissions, and commissions make you richer. You take controversy to the bank.

The overture segues into *Tannhäuser*'s first scene as you perfect Joan's face. You've dispensed with her traditional rosy-cheeked piety and imbued her with a dragon's resolve. Her bedraggled dreadlocks fly in the breeze. She's mud-smeared, blood-smeared, dogged. A woman who kicks ass. The kind you'd want if you were heterosexual. Or bi.

Which makes you think of Cedric.

You've been chastised for being a black-and-white thinker regarding sexuality, but the gray realm of bisexuality annoys you. Bisexuals are sellouts who lie to themselves—and the world—in an irresponsibly selfish effort to keep at least one foot in acceptable society. You neither trust bisexuals, nor believe such a thing truly exists. You'd never get seriously involved with one.

And yet.

The thumb that grazed Cedric's neck is, at the moment, smudged with oil paint, but you can't forget the feel, the texture, of those scars. What is it about him? He is not your equal—not in education, class, money, or the use of grammar.

And yet.

At first it was that glowing solitude. But during coffee yesterday you saw something underneath: Fire. And resolve. Perhaps the kind you're painting into Joan. The kind that empowers one to spar with an intimidating, giddily controversial artist and rack up a few good jabs. You prize friction—in all its forms. It makes you feel alive. You were alive yesterday with Cedric Curtis.

The Act One duet between Tannhäuser and the goddess Venus blooms to a crescendo. It's the famous—at the time infamous—1961 live Bayreuth Festival performance with Grace Bumbry as Venus. She thrusts her ringing mezzo up and over the orchestra with the ease of a swan as you apply the final brushstroke. Joan is done. You've planned a hookup to celebrate. Blaine: a black, mustached cosmetics chemist who works out twice a day and looks nothing like his forty-four years. Blaine is a would-be digital entrepreneur in the throes of launching a cosmetics line. You'll meet for a drink at a place in Chelsea that fools itself and its patrons into believing it's a gay sports bar because ESPN plays on its TVs and the shirtless bartenders wear Yankees caps. After a drink or three—you'll have to treat Blaine, he's always broke—you'll head to your penthouse, smoke weed, and fuck all night. He'll likely ask you to invest in his cosmetics business. You hope he waits until morning. Saying *hell no* is easier after coffee.

Your phone buzzes. A text from Cedric.

need to talk

You don't hesitate.

My place.

You give him the address, text Blaine to cancel, rush home, and inform the doorman you're expecting a guest and to send him on up.

"Sure, Mr. Crane. No problem," the doorman says.

Beneath his pert and practiced smile, you sense a *wink-wink*. The doormen are used to your hookups, your rent boys, your fuck buddies. They aren't dense. You picture them behind the lobby desk, poring over their phones, propping their bored heads on balled-up fists. They take one look at the muscles and tight jeans swinging toward them, wave the guy to the elevator, and resume phone surfing.

You shower, dress, ogle yourself in the mirror. *Adore* is a more accurate term. You're extremely attractive and you know it. It's difficult to believe that there was a time you didn't.

The first fifteen years of your life you were skinny. No one hesitated to hurl more colorful terms your way—*lanky, gaunt*—as well as more startling ones—*scrawny, bony, starved, emaciated.* As if people felt obliged to ensure you cherished no delusions of being attractive. They took that obligation seriously. If you had a dollar for each time a bully—child, adult, cousin, grandparent—reminded you that you were skinny, you'd have enough to start a bank. If you counted each time Justine said, *Clean that plate—you're nothing but skin and bones*, you'd run out of numbers. Your skinniness bothered people. Decades later, you know why: The worst sin a man can commit is not being man enough. Not good at sports? You're not man enough. Don't want to fuck women? You're not man enough. Rather sew than mow the lawn? Not man enough. And if you're skinny, you are literally not man enough.

It wasn't merely your sinful lack of weight that offended people. Your quietness, your disdain for and dismissal of popular culture, and your affinity for boys, vexed them as mightily. They took all those bricks, stacked them side by side and one on top of the other until they walled you off. They made you an outcast. They made you bitter. They made you self-sufficient. Self-sufficiency spawned thick skin. Thick skin deflected the pain of existing behind a wall. At fifteen you were forced to lift weights in P.E. Your dread was immense, as was your shock when your body blew up. You hadn't expected results, much less superior ones. The muscle spread fast, unstoppable as forest fire. Gawking at yourself in the mirror became an addiction as pleasurable as masturbating. You loved stripping off your clothes, modeling in the full-length mirror on the back of your bedroom door. Like you're doing right now. You loved loving yourself. After fifteen years of being told you had no right to.

The doorbell rings.

You stare at Cedric in the doorway. His lip busted, bleeding.

Cheeks and forehead stained with bruises. He holds his arm like it's broken.

You yank him inside, sit him down, run for Neosporin, bandages, a cool, wet cloth. As you administer to him, tears collect in his eyes, but do not spill. His body shudders with the effort of holding them back. His bloodied lip quivers. Both fists clamp tight as if strangling something. You want to say, *let go*, but you admire the strength that allows him to keep it together.

You clean him up, make him drink wine. The two of you sit in silence. You stop yourself from commanding him to tell you what happened. He came here. He chose to come here, to you. He'll tell you when he's ready. But you want revenge on whoever did this. You grind your teeth as your fury accelerates, as the tempest of protectiveness that overwhelmed you when you saw the scars threatens to squall again.

You put an opera on. What else is there to do? *Ariadne auf Naxos*, your favorite Richard Strauss composition. You're uncertain Cedric will like it—Strauss can be an acquired taste—but this recording stars Jessye Norman and who in his correct mind doesn't idolize Ms. Jessye Norman?

The music and wine lull him. The room is tranquil, but tingling with things unsaid, with tensions unarticulated, unacted on. He's up, limping around, taking in the room, perusing the art, your library of books, music, and films, the gallery of wines and spirits behind the antique mahogany bar. You watch him. You enjoy watching him. You smile. He's skinny. You like that.

"Where do you live, my dear?"

"I told you yesterday: Jackson Heights."

"That's in Queens, yes?" you say.

"That's in Queens, yes."

You pick up the crystal vase you purchased on your last trip to Amsterdam and haul your arm back as if to launch it at him. "Smart ass. You've mistaken me for someone who ventures outside Manhattan."

"Aw, come on, man. Don't tell me you're one of *those* Manhattan people, who think the boroughs is countryside."

"I've visited Brooklyn. The gentrified parts."

"So as far as you're concerned," Cedric says, "if you got to cross a bridge or go under a river to get there, you don't need to get there."

"Smart boy."

"I did good in school."

"You did *well* in school."

"That's what I said."

"I meant—" You sigh. You're so glad he's here.

"Come here, Cedric. Sit." Once again that arousal when he obeys. Your dick commences a slow-rage to hardness. "Tell me what happened today. Now."

"Got my ass kicked."

"That much is obvious, my dear. Who kicked it? And why?"

"Dude named Leland. Friend of Mel's."

The girl he told you about yesterday. Apparently, the type who attracts competing suitors and violence. You'll not soon forget the first time you watched one of those ridiculous morning "talk" shows where guests literally thrash the homewreckers who have slept with their significant others. You were scandalized, but so titillated you couldn't help but sit forward, as you're doing now.

"Kicking another man's ass," you say, "would seem the role of a boyfriend, not a mere friend."

"Leland ain't her boyfriend. He's a lot older. Drives a Jag. White guy. He . . . helps Mel with her rent."

You're atrocious at math, but it's easy putting two and two together to calculate what's going on with Miss Melanie. You lay a hand on Cedric's bare arm, his sliver of a bicep, and caress it, smoothing your hand up and down his warm skin. For a moment, he lets you.

He gets up, finds his way to one of your most loved possessions: the painting *Morpheus*. A Black man surrounded by night and stars, the moon nesting on his shoulders. An original, signed by the master himself: Myron Hillhouse. Your mentor. Your antagonist. Your competitor. Your once-upon-a-time, once-in-a-while lover. Your friend. Justine loathes him—personally and artistically. Personally since you introduced them during the first iteration of your relationship (*Too old for you. Too flip. I don't like his racial politics.*) and artistically from the second your father gave you Myron's book of paintings when you were a teenager. (*Nothing but gimmicks. He paints these things to get a rise out of people.*) Likewise your half-brother William—whose opinions almost always echo Justine's—denigrates Myron's paintings—and yours—as "politically correct cartoons." But your devotion to Myron eclipses your family's loathing. If Cedric loved him, too, it would mean so much.

He spends minutes gazing at the painting, buried in it. Not unlike the first time you saw *Morpheus* in the book your father gave you. Of all the paintings, it enthralled you the most lushly. You were an art star by the time it was auctioned off in an estate sale. You snapped it up without thought to the exorbitant cost. Sitting next to you as the auctioneer droned on, and the price soared higher, and you kept raising your hand to cinch the bid, was Myron.

"Is this you?" Cedric asks.

"Is *who* me?"

"Guy in the painting. Looks like you. Built like you. Thought maybe you posed for it."

The *guy in the painting* is the Greek god of sleep and dreams whom Myron has depicted as beautiful, half-naked, and with the physique of a Black Chippendales dancer. You're shocked at how flattered you feel, shocked part of you is still that skinny kid who couldn't love himself until he had a body the world approved of.

"No, that isn't me. But thank you."

"He looks kind. Like he'd protect you if he could."

You feel the same. As a walled-off kid, you took comfort in the god's gentleness, fantasized about resting in his strong, Black arms, how shielded you'd feel, how cared for.

It's not that late—only eight or so—but the penthouse is dim. It looks almost like night inside. The scars on Cedric's neck

153

stand out, even in the dimness. You wrap your arms around him from behind, bury your face in his neck. You're a foot taller, you have to squat. You scour his neck with your face. The assortment of scars—their textures—surprises and delights you. Some soft, pulpy; others mildly coarse.

"This," you say. "What happened?"

"Second grade. Boy named Dean. Testing out a plastic knife from the cafeteria. Wanted to see how sharp it was. Used the back of my neck for a cutting board. I used to sit at the girls' table at lunch. Dean told the teacher it ain't matter that he cut my neck 'cause I wasn't nothing but a boy who sat with the girls. He got expelled, but slashing the back of my neck became a class game. My daddy said to fight. My mom said to look them in the eye real serious and that would make them stop. I couldn't do either one. The teacher moved my desk next to hers so she could keep an eye on me. *Cedric's a baby*, kids said. *Cedric needs Miss Carson to protect him. Cedric won't fight for his own neck.*"

Unbelievable. Except it isn't. Children rank among the cruelest people. You want to tell him you understand, that you had awful childhood experiences, too. But his experience trounces yours, and your childhood hurts seem void compared to what this boy has told you. You try but cannot think of a single response that won't sound canned. You're lucky: your damage hides under untarnished skin and muscle mass. But Cedric's lives in full display. It will never fade.

"You know what it's like to be treated bad, Paul?" he says. "No. Look at you. You couldn't know."

He does not see you. He sees a famous artist. He sees a handsome, wealthy man. But he does not see *you*. He cannot transmit x-ray vision beneath the crust of you and view the layers of damaged soil. You decide you need to keep it that way.

"Know who did fight for my neck?" Cedric says. "Mel. Protected me like she was a fucking lioness and I was her cub."

"You were in school together?"

"Yeah. She was good to me. Till she figured out how damn pretty she was."

And now the tears he's been holding fall. His body quakes as his whimpers turn into groans and his groans swell into yowls. You hold him through the entire storm. When he quiets, you kiss his neck. Kiss him there. And there. And there. And there.

"I'm glad you're here, Cedric."

"Same."

6.

Mel.

'Sup, girl? Can't believe it's been three months. I decided not to reach out first. Hoped you would. Hurts deep that you didn't. Think about you all the damn time. Wonder if you're still with Leland. Don't know why you sell yourself. Wish you'd let me take care of you. Yeah, I know: you want things and Leland can give them to you and I can't.

But that's changing. I got lots to tell you, girl.

I been seeing Paul. He likes me. And I like him. Kinda.

I went to him the day you let Leland kick my ass. You should see his place. A fuckin' penthouse on the Upper West Side. Building even got a doorman. A fuckin' palace. Big ol' bar right in his living room, and I ain't talking about no rickety folding table with a couple bottles of PBR. I had told him about my ghetto-ass computer with the bootleg software. Next morning he took me to breakfast and Best Buy. He asked me which laptop I wanted. Told him it didn't matter 'cause I ain't have money for one. He said to use the credit card he gave me. So now I got me a up-to-date computer with all the software I wanted. Latest versions, too. Licensed and everything.

There was a time when I would have said, *No, I ain't gonna use that card. I ain't gonna let him do that for me.* I mean, I did use it to buy them flowers, but a damn computer? But something happened when you let Leland throw me down them stairs. Something changed. *I* changed. The world been treating me like shit all my life. The world's done what it wanted to me, taken what it wanted from me. Why shouldn't I get what I want,

155

take what I can for a change? That's what *you* do, Mel. You take everything you can from Leland, from all the others. You take what little I give you. You take and you take and you take. Look at me, giving and giving and loving you and all I get is my ass kicked.

It's time for me to take what I want.

Paul does stuff for me. He takes me to stuff. Opera. Symphony. Jazz clubs. He got me a job, too. Friend of his owns a restaurant in Harlem. Hired me as a host. And Paul put me in school. A certificate program: Web Design and Corporate Desktop Publishing. I'm learning HTML, Photoshop, web programming. Fancy, right? Paul's making it happen. I been tinkering on that piece of shit computer, dreaming about being a web designer. It ain't a dream no more. Dreams ain't nothing but fantasies. But goals is solid. Ain't nothing better than pursuing a goal you're hungry for, and let me tell you something, Mel: I'm hungry, and Paul Crane's feeding me, and I'ma eat every delicious thing he puts on his penthouse table.

You might think I'm using him, that I don't care about him. Ain't true. Paul came into my life out of nowhere and turned it around. And even when we fight I know he gives a shit. Maybe we fight *because* he gives a shit. I was a mess after Leland. Paul fixed me up. He held me. Let me cry on his chest. Let me be the little spoon in bed. First time I did anything like that. All my other times with guys were hookups: slam-bam, we're done, put your clothes on, come on, hurry, my wife'll be back soon, thank you kindly, see you around maybe. This was the first time I laid in a guy's arms. Talked in bed. Spent the night. First time I didn't get off. First time it wasn't about getting off. First time I truly surrendered. First time I wanted to. Paul did that for me. Now he wants to give me the world. Why shouldn't I let him? Ain't no harm in caring 'bout someone *and* getting what you want from them. Give and take. Makes the world go around, right?

And it ain't like he ain't getting plenty from me. He gets someone to talk to about opera. He gets a cute boy who'll keep him young. He gets someone he can mold and shape and say,

Look at him. Look at Cedric. I did that. I built that.

He's so good to me, Mel. Treats me like a prince. But he's intense. I have to make myself keep up. He does everything a thousand-and-one percent. He's disciplined as hell. Works out every morning at five. Runs three times a week. Reads a fuck-ton—always got at least two or three books going at the same time. Keeps up with politics like he's running for president. And don't get me started on his painting. It consumes him. It's almost all he thinks about.

Paul Crane knows his worth. It's what I appreciate 'bout him most. That's what he's teaching me—to know my worth.

He's good to me, but he ain't always good.

Paul's arrogant. He looks down on people who ain't got as much money, or if he thinks they ain't sophisticated, or if they don't know what he knows or like what he likes. If I tell him, "Paul, to each his own," he'll smile and shake his head like I'm a kid saying cute, dumb things.

Paul loves getting up on a high horse and talking down to me. Like when I said we should hang out at my place in JH and he said ain't nothing in Queens worth his while, and I said, "*I'm* in Queens, *I'm* worth your while," and he said something 'bout enjoying the fresh country breezes in the outer boroughs.

Paul's always judging me 'cause I'm young. Says stuff like, "You millennials don't know anything," and, "You'll learn one day that the world's not waiting for you to show up."

Paul loves telling me what to do, giving orders like he's my sergeant or something. I liked it at first. You know, this big, older, famous man telling me what to do—it turned me on. I think it turned him on, too. It was a game we both got off on. But now it don't feel like no game. There's a hard edge to it, sometimes a sharp one. Before, it wasn't no big deal if I didn't do what he said. Now, part of me wonders what'll happen if I don't.

Paul's an asshole. He ain't introduced me to none of his friends, not one, except the guy who owns the restaurant. He goes to parties or dinners and don't take me with him. He has dinners at his place and he'll say, "Come over after eleven," when he knows the guests'll be gone.

Paul's embarrassed by my clothes. He hates hoodies, I mean *hates*. At least on Black dudes. He sees a Black dude in one and he can't stop scowling, but a cute white guy walks by rocking a hoodie, he drools. I told him, you don't like my clothes, buy me some new shit. So he took me to, like, ten stores and bought me shirts, shoes, shorts, pants, jackets. I don't like all the new stuff, but I wear it and he still don't introduce me to people.

What the fuck am I supposed to do with that?

Paul's ashamed of me. The way I talk. He corrects me all the time. He gets mad when I say *ain't*; when I say *ax* instead of *ask*. His sarcasm is a knife. We was talking 'bout something this one time and I didn't get his point. I said, "Give me a good example. Be pacific." His eyes got small, like he was zeroing in on me and he said, "How could I possibly be the largest, deepest body of water on Earth? I'm better off being Atlantic."

Would he correct a white guy who said *ain't*? Would he criticize wrong English coming out of a white mouth?

7.

The blond waiter walks by and flirts another smile at you. For the last hour he's been smiling and winking and doing little things to get your attention while he works. His protuberant backside and bright skin make him attractive, but not as intriguing as his coworker, an older waiter—mid to late fifties?—whose hair is swept in waves of brown strewn with splinters of silver; beard a gauze of brown fur on a rugged, lined face that denotes a sexy wear-and-tear. His posture is taut and dignified. He has a slight gut, but it works on his build. The blond waiter keeps flirting, but the older one gets your vote.

You sit with a glass of sherry while the waiters stride around the penthouse, preparing for tonight's cocktail party. A relatively small affair. Twenty people. Some artist colleagues, a couple of gallery owners, a Broadway actress, a few Upper East Side trust fund babies, and miscellaneous glitterati and supposed influencers who do god-knows-what other than attend cocktail parties.

Once again you did not invite Cedric. Once again you should feel guilty about it. And, once again, you do not. Your young beau isn't ready. If your acquaintances and colleagues meet a boy incapable of forming a grammatically correct sentence, your reputation will suffer. The gossip would sting.

Paul Crane's boy from the hood.

A sugar daddy arrangement, right?

Paul's attempt at street cred, so people stop saying he's Black in name only.

You've never been involved with anyone like Cedric. What does that mean? *Like Cedric?* Does it mean Black? No. You've been with Black men. Admittedly the number of white men who populate your life exceeds that of Black, but you're not the kind of shallow gay man who sees beauty exclusively in one type; the kind who defends his disdain for anyone outside that type by claiming it's "just a preference." So what does *like Cedric* mean? You know, but refuse to articulate the shameful thought in your head. You take a sip of sherry so you don't have to.

"Mr. Crane?"

The blond waiter leans against the bar, a hip poking out, his attempt at seduction. You want to snicker. He's ludicrous.

"We're all set up," he says. "Ready to receive your guests."

What else are you ready to receive?

You could have him right now, bend him over and have your way with him and he wouldn't go all #MeToo on you. You don't act on it, but the knowledge is empowering.

"Thank you," you say.

He remains against the bar, pokes his hip out another few inches, and heaves a nonchalant yawn. After a minute passes and you don't ask him to suck your dick, he says, "Taylor and me will be in the kitchen."

Taylor and I will be in the kitchen.

So Taylor's the other one's name. Handsome name, handsome man. You don't ask this one's name. You drain the last drop of sherry and go upstairs to prepare for tonight.

First stop: your closet, which is larger than a Manhattan rail-road apartment. Pants, shirts, suits, and ties in one eternal row on the left, shoes on the right. Three full-length mirrors stationed in strategic spots. A cushioned bench so you can try on shoes. Track lighting above. A vanity with a mirror and Hollywood lights. A dorm-sized refrigerator filled with bottles of water so you don't have to carry them all the way from downstairs.

You quickly decide on a pair of black slacks—the designer is a friend. The rest is more complicated. The choice of shirt will influence the shoes and belt. And your watch needs to comply with the whole ensemble. You consider a leopard-patterned satin shirt with mother-of-pearl buttons and black shoes with patches of leopard that echo the shirt. But the leopard shirt is too much: you don't want to give in to the stereotype of Blacks wearing "wild" patterns. Since the leopard shirt is out, so are the shoes, and you have to start over, this time with a red silk shirt, but you wore that recently so it goes back on the hanger and a midnight blue shirt steps up as the next candidate. But you want to wear a black blazer. Midnight blue will not provide enough of a color contrast so it goes back on the hanger, too. How about the red and grey-striped shirt? The material is sheer. Your chest will be visible, nipples, chest hair, and all. This shirt works well with the black blazer so it's a keeper. The red croco-dile-skin shoes mirror the red in the shirt and add flash. So will your gold-and-diamond watch.

There. Done. Decided. And as usual, the process is torture. Not the choosing—that's second nature, like selecting the best colors and textures for a painting. It's having to be perfect that infuriates you. Having to make sure each and every element is impeccable, and not only with your clothing. The hors d'oeuvres. The wines. The music. The guest list itself. As a Black man, there is no room for error. But the devastating thing is this: when you get everything right—and you always do—you're the exception. You are a talented, successful, articulate Black man and you are considered the exception, not the rule. You make a mistake in any arena and it reflects not only on you, but on the entire race. So you don't make mistakes. This is something you're trying to teach Cedric.

You recall an incident from childhood when Justine picked you up from school. Your jacket was tied around your waist. You had only half-stepped into the car when she let loose. "That's sloppy," she said. "Slovenly. How you groom yourself, and every-thing else you do, reflects on me, on your father, and on every other Black person." You countered by insisting all the kids wore their jackets like that. "All the kids aren't Black," Justine said, and that ended that discussion—permanently. In the forty years since, you have never once tied a jacket around your waist.

You soak in the tub, dress, and an hour later the party is in full swing.

Everyone fawns over the Broadway actress. She's starring in a mega-hit revival of *The Wiz*. You enjoyed it so much you bought the cast album, an anomaly since Broadway music isn't generally your taste. There's buzz she may get the Tony. She's beautiful, thirty, and bisexual, so some of both the male and female guests hope they have a chance with her. The trust fund babies work the room. Their parents left them enough money to render work unnecessary, but not enough to call themselves *rich*, so they hobnob with the wealthy guests in a strained effort at relevance. The artists segregate themselves off to the side to observe and snicker and babble pithy comments about the oth-ers. You've done the same thing—stood on the sidelines to judge and critique and look down on the forlorn souls who aren't as enlightened and above it all.

Your most interesting and possibly most dangerous guest is a gay society reporter from a conservative website that typically disparages your work. (*Crane's disrespectful rendering of Elizabeth I as Black represents everything wrong with minority artists' mis-guided attempts at so-called multiculturalism. Their stated claim is the desire to level the cultural playing field, but in reality, they're assaulting the public with politically correct falsehoods that make a mockery of blessed historical fact.*) He isn't here in his official reporter capacity, but his eyes and ears are no doubt primed to snag any tidbit that can be finagled into a damaging headline. You wonder if he knows your half-brother. William is an attorney and a prominent star in conservative legal circles. He frequently contributes gleefully scathing Antonin Scalia-style op-eds to the website this reporter writes for. The guests have separated into cliques, and the reporter drifts from one to another, speaking a little, but mostly observing, listening. He reminds you of the silent maids in nineteenth-century Gothic novels—the ones who seem invisible but are adroit in the art of intelligence-gathering. You occasionally catch him turning his back, removing a small notebook from his jacket's inside pocket, and scribbling quick notes. Those scribbles make you nervous. You invited this archconservative in a mischievous effort to mix it up with your mostly liberal guests. You hope you haven't gone too far.

The blond waiter continues his smiling and winking. Taylor catches him, looks at you, shakes his head. You already liked Taylor. You like him more now. You wink at Taylor. He winks back.

The party is rolling along when Cedric comes wading through the guests on his way to you. He's wearing the light blue polo, black slacks, and beige oxfords you bought him last week. Not exactly cocktail party attire, but he looks good, upbeat, self-assured. It's partly the clothes, but mostly the new aura of confidence that's been taking shape around him, one you feel justified in taking credit for. But this brightening confidence scares you, too. What happens when it outshines you? What happens when and if he no longer needs you?

The guests scrutinize him and turn to each other with inquisitive faces and whispered questions. Despite its cliquishness, the group has bonded and is wary of anyone new. The observers on the outskirts join the rest, curious as everyone else about this newcomer.

"Hey," Cedric says to you.

"Hello. How are you this evening?"

Your formality hurts him. He takes a small step backward, rubs the back of his neck. The brightening confidence clouds

162

over. The room is silent as your guests await an introduction.

"I thought you worked tonight," you say.

"Restaurant was slow. They let me go early."

You're angry. He shouldn't be here. But look at him: handsome, smart, gentle, and yours. You open your arms wide and he sails into them. You're so glad he's here.

"This is Cedric," you announce. You snap your fingers at the blond waiter. "Bring him a drink." The waiter frowns and complies. When serving Cedric, he turns his nose up.

You put your arm around Cedric's shoulders and he puts his around your waist.

The actress says, "Are the two of you . . . ?"

"Yes," you say, are proud to say. You bend down, take his face in your hands and kiss him.

The guests make small talk with Cedric, ask him questions which he answers mostly with *yes*, *no*, or short, quiet sentences. You catch Taylor's eye. He nods toward the blond waiter who stands at attention on the periphery, pouting. Taylor winks at you. You wink back.

Everything is going fine. The guests are enchanted by—and, in some cases, jealous of—the young man who has captured the heart of the planet's biggest art star. Even the reporter nods and smiles what looks like approval. All is well until one of the trust fund babies asks, "Where do you live, Cedric?" You know she's nosing for trouble when she adds, "Which part of Manhattan?"

"Jackson Heights," he says. He looks up at you and says, "Queens," as if challenging you and everyone in the room. The general reaction is one of polite disillusionment, but also triumph because they've discovered a flaw in this diamond. Your fingers are set lightly on his neck. You feel the muscles lock.

"I like it there," he says, so defensively the trust fund baby and a few others wince. "Ain't nowhere else I wanna live. There's a lot of electricity in JH. You get off the train and walk down to the street and—"

"Ohhh," someone says. "Walk *down* to the street. An elevated train."

"It's an outer borough thing," someone else says. Snickers prickle through the crowd.

Cedric is undeterred. "You get off the train in JH and there's all these people from all these different countries, countries I ain't never heard of. One time I heard someone say they don't like going to Queens 'cause they ain't feel like they was in America. But I go walking through JH and see all those people and I'm like, yo, I'd love to go to some of these countries that these people be from. And one day I'll get there. Ain't no doubt. Maybe this famous artist will take me."

Eyes have been flicking at you all through his monologue. The trust fund baby covers her mouth with her hand. Without turning his back, the reporter retrieves his notebook and begins scribbling. The blond waiter smiles large. The actress tries to change the subject, but the damage is done.

The reporter is first to announce his departure. Everyone else follows suit until only you, Cedric, and the waiters are left.

You pour a drink and deflate into a chair. Cedric remains standing, a few feet in front of you, like a subordinate standing at the desk of a furious boss.

"I should have texted," Cedric says, "but I wanted to see you. If I texted, you would've told me to come after everyone was gone. You ain't never had me to one of your parties."

"No, Cedric. I ain't."

The waiters tiptoe as they gather up lipstick-stained wineglasses, party napkins, and crystal saucers holding the remains of *petit fours*. If you see a hint of a smirk on the blond's face, you'll punch him.

"There was a society reporter here," you say. "I can imagine tomorrow morning's write-up. You're correct: you should have texted before you came."

"Yeah, of course I should have. And you would've said, *Don't come over, Cedric, 'cause you was born in a Bronx hood and you live in shitty Queens and you worked in a bodega and you don't speak Harvard English and if people see you with me, it'll remind them that I'm Black and I can't have that.* Am I right? Am I right, Paul Crane?"

164

Your lack of response is answer enough. Cedric leaves.

You sit, motionless, while the waiters finish up. Blondie leaves. Taylor hovers behind.

"Mr. Crane, it's been a pleasure," he says. He continues to hover. You've already paid the bill, which included lofty tips, so that can't be what he's waiting for.

"What do you want, Taylor?"

"Danny's taking the equipment back. I'd like to apologize for his behavior. He's too cute for his own good. Got a bad habit of throwing himself at handsome hosts. Anyway. We're all done and, like I said, Danny's taking the equipment back and I was wondering, oh, I don't know, if you'd like some company this evening. Ha. Now who's throwing himself at the handsome host?"

You laugh. "Pour yourself a drink, Taylor. Make yourself at home. Take your shoes off. Take mine off while you're at it."

8.

I thought it'd be good to see you today, Mel. When you called this morning and said it'd been too long, you missed me, wanted to see me, I said to hell with classes and headed straight to your place. Hearing from you gave me hope. And I needed some.

Ain't talked to Paul in two weeks. He ain't called or texted, and I ain't either. I been going to classes that he's paying for, though. And I still got the job he got me. I miss him. But when you texted, Mel, I couldn't help thinking you and me could be together again. I know better than to get ahead of myself. Daddy used to warn me, "Baby, God don't like it one bit when you count your chickens before they're hatched. Be careful. He'll make sure you end up with a shitload of cracked eggs."

When I got to your place you looked so pretty. Smelled pretty, too. Leland probably bought the perfume but it didn't matter 'cause your arms around my neck was good and my hands around your waist was good and next thing I knew we was in the bedroom and I didn't know how we got there, whether we walked or flew. So long since we'd been together. So long since I'd been with a girl. I was nervous. Took me a little while to settle in to it. To settle in to you.

Mel. Melanie. My girl.

We was each other's first time. High school, junior year. First time *and* with someone I loved? I took that shit serious. Shit like that's supposed to last forever. Would have, too, if you hadn't figured out how pretty you was.

That was the worst thing ever happened to us.

But here I was, with you after so many months, us lying there, kissing and laughing, me thinking 'bout happiness, how there ain't no such thing, how the best you can hope for is to be content. Lying there with you, I was. I was OK with never making the jump to happiness. I was at a place that was good as got. I wasn't about to fuck it up by getting greedy. I was drifting along in that good place when you said, "Leland broke it off." You cuddled up closer. "At least I still got you, Cedric."

At least.

At least I still got you, Cedric.

Your face was against the side of my neck. Your breasts spilled across my chest. My hand was in your hair. I closed my eyes and dug down as deep as I could, looking for the most jagged blade I could find. Took a minute, but I found it.

"Yup," I said. "At least you got me. Hos always got a backup."

You sat up. I'll never forget the look on your face, like you was trying to figure out if I was for real or not. And I'll never forget the slap across my face after you realized I was.

I rubbed my face, got out of bed to get my clothes, and said, "You still slap hard, girl. And them fake nails is still sharp."

9.

You haven't seen him in weeks. He hasn't called or texted and you're suffering. You wake in the morning and remain in bed brooding instead of heading to the gym. You don't paint. You don't go out. You don't hook up. When Taylor the waiter pinged you with an arousing selfie and invited himself over, you replied, *Not today, thank you.* But you knew it was bad when Blaine the chemist asked you to invest in his enterprise and, too bereft to expend the effort to refuse, you agreed. You're now a 5 percent silent partner in a venture you have absolute faith will implode in six months.

You're in an Uber, crossing the Queensboro Bridge on your way to Jackson Heights. You need your face in Cedric's neck. You need your face in all of him.

The driver drops you in front of a five-story brown brick apartment building with all the charm of a housing project. So. This is Queens. You've lived in New York well over twenty years and, aside from flying out of LaGuardia or JFK or crossing Queens to get to the Hamptons, you've never set foot in this borough. But Cedric was right about the electricity. Shops up and down the street selling everything from cell phones to clothing to bongs. Restaurants serving food from across the globe—Indian, Bolivian, Romanian, Ethiopian. A culinary United Nations. And people, everywhere, cramming corners and storefronts, whirling to and fro in every direction, chattering in a multitude of languages, sporting Western dress as well as the traditional garb of their home countries. You stand outside Cedric's building, take it all in, and decide you've been too harsh. You'd never leave Manhattan, but you see the appeal of this place.

You step into the vestibule and press "5C" on the intercom.

"Yeah, who is it?"

"It's me, my dear."

There's silence before he says, "No shit," and buzzes you in.

Good thing you're fit because there's no elevator—you have to hike all the way to the fifth floor. The building is clean, if a bit stale-smelling. Once inside the apartment, you find faded, threadbare rugs scattered on hazy wood floors and furniture that looks like it was rescued from a thrift shop. Music plays, shining some cheer on this murky home—a collection of virtuoso *bel canto* arias sung by the tenor Lawrence Brownlee, an acquaintance. You turned Cedric on to it after taking him to see Lawrence in *Il Barbiere di Siviglia*. You love that he's listening to music you recommended.

"Desmond Paul Crane, Jr. in Queens?" he says. "You must really fucking miss me."

You and Cedric dive into a tight, needy, ravenous embrace. You hold him by the neck, his face to your chest, kiss the top of his head over and over and over as you relax for the first time in weeks. You have your boy back.

The embrace melts. He steps out of your arms. Something is different, awkward. You've fought before and made up before, picking up where you left off, falling back into your plush Paul-and-Cedric rhythm. Something tells you it won't be that way this time. Something in his eyes. They're kitten-soft and beaming love, but there's a hardness there, too. A warning: *Careful. I'm only going to take so much of your bullshit from now on.*

It's not only his eyes that are different. His smell, too. Like perfume. He reeks of it. He's been with that girl. Melanie. You're sure of it. You've hooked up with a sizable cadre of men since you've been with Cedric, but his being with Melanie feels like betrayal.

"Pack a bag," you say. "Come back to the city. We'll have dinner and go home. My place, I mean. Which I hope you think of as home."

It's the most intimate thing you've ever said to anyone. It gives you a rush that leaves you woozy.

"We'll have dinner in the neighborhood," he says, "and go to Manhattan after."

"*This* neighborhood?"

"Yes, Paul. This neighborhood."

"But I'm sure you'd rather—"

"Paul: This. Neighborhood."

Something is definitely different. He's stood up to you before, but now he's standing his ground, which is not the same thing. The two overlap, of course, each bleeding across the other, blotting the already sketchy lines between self-defense and self-assertiveness. Cedric has often stood up to you to inform you that you're full of shit. Now he's standing his ground to inform you that he is not. The difference unnerves you. A new layer has been added to your gratifyingly contentious relationship. You're uncertain what to make of it, but have no choice but to play along until you can gauge how to navigate this new layer, how to circumvent it.

"I need to shower," Cedric says. "Make yourself at home."

You wander around the apartment. There's only one bedroom, and it belongs to the roommate. You recall that Cedric sleeps on the futon, that the living room is essentially his bedroom. He's made it his own to the extent that's possible. His books are on the shelf, his computer on the vinyl-topped folding table. The room is tidy and organized, which you've come to expect from him.

You've settled on the futon to enjoy Lawrence's singing when a phone buzzes. At least you assume it's a phone. Ringtones are so creative these days, who knows? Cedric's phone lies on the table, lit up with an incoming text—from Melanie. You grab the phone, open the message. He's an intelligent boy, but pretty dumb not to password-protect his phone.

> sorry about earlier really love you want to be with you call me

You act quickly. You tap *reply* and type:

> we aint right for each other we see the world different dont want to see you no more go fuck yourself

You delete her message and manipulate the settings to block everything from her number. But not before saving her number in your own phone.

Cedric comes out of the bathroom, drying himself, dick dangling sweetly. God you've missed him.

"There's a Indian place around the corner," he says, drying his hairless underarms. "You'll like it." He says this as if he's made the decision for you.

You take your naked boy in your arms, kiss him, cradle his damp head with the cup of your hand, press his face into your chest again, fondle his scars. Lawrence Brownlee croons an intricate coloratura passage from *Barbiere*. You catch sight of Cedric's phone sitting oh so innocently on the table.

"Yes, my dear," you tell him. "I'll like it. I promise."

10.

She's fifteen minutes late.

Your anxiety that she won't show is tempered by the assumption that her curiosity will be so great, she'll be unable to resist. But you're impatient because you want to have done with this business. It has to be executed with immaculate precision. You can't afford a single loose end.

You have never been this nervous. You've schemed before. You've lied, manipulated, dissembled—maneuvered, conspired, connived. But this is the one and only time your hands have trembled when preparing to engage in an intrigue. This isn't like you. You take pride in your steady hands, fingers abiding and reliable as they grasp a paintbrush. Not these trembling things that can't hold the menu of this bougie Park Slope, Brooklyn, restaurant. Demographically, Park Slope is worlds away from Cedric's Jackson Heights. It lacks that neighborhood's verve. Park Slope reminds you of the Upper East Side: attractive, but sterile; orderly, yet soulless.

Your hands are no steadier as you clutch the cut-glass water goblet, a sunny lemon wedge fastened on its rim. *What if Cedric finds out?* The question, the danger, have clattered through your mind like pinballs.

You check your watch. Twenty-five minutes late. You consider texting, but fear she may perceive that as desperation, which could weaken your hand. This business requires you to show as tough—and steady—a hand as possible. Trembling will not do. *But what happens if Cedric finds out?* The pinballs clatter again. You consider abandoning this risky scheme. The consequence of failure is monumental. But the benefit—and allure—of success is exceptional. You calm yourself with that.

You're about to check your watch again when you see a young woman in a summer dress—floral, floor-length, strapless—speaking with the host, who points you out.

She's prettier than you thought she'd be. You had pictured light skin, a model-thin body, pomegranate breasts. But she sports the sultry, buxom contours of Marilyn Monroe, the exquisite dark brown tint of Alfre Woodard. It makes sense that someone attracted to women would be drawn to her, but as she makes her way to your table, you're struck by something else: How much she reminds you of Justine. Not physically, so much—Justine is and has always been slim, not buxom, and her complexion isn't quite as dark—but there is something in this girl's bearing that echoes your mother. The fluid elegance in her glide to the table; both the subtlety and boldness with which she has applied her makeup (light glaze of blush, lips dyed bright as a flare); the aura of fearlessness that makes her stand out like a diva. In the brief time it takes to finish her glide, you recall an evening from long ago, an evening with Justine.

The soprano Barbara Hendricks was giving a recital of Debussy *chansons*, and Justine had tickets, given to her by a colleague who couldn't attend. The two of you went; William was too young. You were eleven. She dressed you in slacks, white shirt, and bow tie, but worried over what to wear herself. Her wardrobe held nothing fancy or formal, and she couldn't afford to go shopping. At one point, she almost gave the tickets away for lack of a suitable dress, but she finally scavenged one from her closet: a satin, sleeveless, rose-colored dress she hadn't worn in years and had forgotten about. "This won't work," she said. "It's out of style." But it was the best she could do. Justine took extra time with her hair and makeup, selected her accessories with the fastidious eye of a museum curator, and when the two of you arrived at the concert hall, your mother may not have been the most glamorously dressed woman there, but she was, by far, the most elegant. She walked into that auditorium, head high, grace in her every stride. Barbara Hendricks swept onstage looking marvelous in a formal gown, but you tittered that your mother was more regal. You were proud of her. You've always been so proud of her.

And now here is a lovely young woman, probably as unlike Justine as she could possibly be, but reflecting her, if only a little.

Always the gentleman, you stand as she arrives at the table. "Melanie! Thank you for coming. Have a seat, please. Waiter! A bottle of Prosecco. Well. Melanie. You're wondering who the hell I am and what this is all about."

"Uh, yeah."

You called her yesterday, introduced yourself as a good friend of Cedric's, and said it was imperative you meet to discuss something critical. She demanded to know how you obtained her number; you told her not to worry about it. Although you blocked her number on his phone, you instructed her not to contact Cedric—a precaution as well as a ploy to rally her curiosity. You planned this meticulously, right down to choosing a day when Cedric has school all day and works all evening. But now that the moment of truth has arrived, massive doubts assail you.

What if this fails? What if I can't convince her? What if Cedric finds out?

The waiter brings the Prosecco. You get to the point: "I care very much for Cedric, as do you, I'm sure. His life, his future, have such potential. He's worked hard to educate himself, improve himself, give himself a fresh start. You have an opportunity to help him with that."

Melanie takes all this in, lifts the Prosecco to her mouth. Her fingernails are lit with the same flaring red on her lips. She eyes you.

"You still ain't told me shit, mister," she says. "You still ain't told me who you are and why we're here."

Her candor makes you tremble again. She won't make this easy. The realization stuns you.

"I am Cedric's friend. A very good friend. I care about him."

"Already said that, mister. Shit don't get clarified just 'cause you repeat it." She looks you over, cocks her head to the right. "You said you're Cedric's friend. What kind of friend?"

Despite your trembling you reach for your Prosecco, causing the flute to quiver. She notices, and it makes you so nervous you drop the flute, spilling Prosecco across the table. The liquid speeds toward her, but she keeps her head cocked and her eyes steady on you. The liquid stops before it reaches her. A passing busboy cleans up the mess, refills your glass from the bottle on the table. A cunning smile floods Melanie's mouth. Your *faux pas* with the Prosecco exposed you. You've given her the upper hand. And she knows it. You underestimated this young woman. You recall Justine: a tenacious woman with her share of flaws and sadness, but someone you misjudge at your peril.

"If you're done spilling shit," Melanie says, "tell me what's going on here."

A cluster of phlegm has accumulated in your throat. You cough to clear it and say, "In order for Cedric to have a truly fresh start, he needs to move on from you. Or rather, *you* need to move on from *him*."

"What the fuck? Some uppity nigger telling me what I need to do?"

Melanie may have meant to level you, but she's evoked yet another memory. You recall Justine telling you how Blacks shamed her because of how she spoke, the music she liked, her conservative politics. *Uppity nigger* was the slur they used. "Did it bother you?" you once asked her. "It bothered me," she answered, "until it didn't. If anything, it empowered me. That slur was confirmation that I was on the right track."

Your hand does not shake when you grasp the refilled flute. "You're not good for him, Melanie. You need to go. I'll give you $25,000 to leave New York, never come back, never speak to or contact Cedric ever again."

There. Good. You've blindsided her. You see it in her wide-open mouth that seems like it may never close again. You think you've retaken control, but she collects herself and replies, "How you know I won't tell Cedric about this?" Her voice, edged with attitude and disdain before, now sounds almost tender.

"Because you want the money more than you want him."

You hope that's true. This entire plan depends on it.

What a convenience having well-placed contacts who owe you favors. Once you'd pilfered the girl's phone number, you reached out to a colleague who knows someone in the telecom industry. That person obtained Melanie's full name and address. Prize information in hand, you contacted a high-ranking state official—for whom you raised a hoard of money to put her over the top in a bloodletting runoff election—and learned that Melanie Sheniqua Baker's rent is several months in arrears. She'll have no choice but to accept your offer—and the conditions that go with it. You hope.

She takes a dainty sip of Prosecco. "$50,000."

You predicted she'd double the price. You built the doubling into the budget. "Agreed!"

Done. Your future with Cedric is now clear of its peskiest obstacle. You think about calling your friend who owns the restaurant and asking him to give Cedric the night off so you can celebrate with your sweet boy. You feel relieved and animated, almost light-headed. *Mission accomplished*, you think, until Melanie says, "That's a down payment. Want me to stay away, you're going to have to give me a little something extra. Every month."

"How much is *a little something?*"

"$5,000."

"*Every month?* You're crazy."

"Fine. I'll tell Cedric."

Yes, her number is blocked on Cedric's phone. But she must know where he lives. She's surely in touch with mutual friends who can reach him.

Goddamn it.

The $5,000 is not the issue—you spend three times that amount each month on clothes, restaurants, and opera tickets. It's the idea of being under this girl's thumb in perpetuity, the fact that you've created a situation intended to give you control and you fucked it up. You have no choice here. You've lost control. At least until you can neutralize Miss Melanie Sheniqua Baker.

"Aren't we a little gold digger?" you say. "Cedric did mention that. Well. There we are. Let's shake on it."

You extend a hand across the table. Melanie looks at it, sips her Prosecco.

11.

I graduated today, Mel. Not a real graduation with a cap and gown and marching across a stage. This school ~~don't have no~~ doesn't have a graduation ceremony if you're ~~getting~~ earning a certificate. I'm proud anyway. I'd like to think you'd be proud of me. Paul is.

I'm looking for a job. I want to work in ~~a~~ an office. ~~I ain't never had no office job before.~~ I've never worked in an office. I've always been a cashier or a delivery guy or worked in a restaurant. Now I can do better, be better. Marketable skills. That's what Paul calls what I have now. You should be proud of me, Mel. But I know you won't be. It's not in you. There was a time when it was. Back before you knew you were pretty. But it's OK. Because it's in Paul. Paul is everything to me that you should have been, and I'm thankful every single day for him. This ~~ain't~~ isn't the relationship I wanted, or expected. But it's the one I've got. And I will make the most of it. Because you know what? People do what they want to get what they want. They don't give a shit about ~~nothing~~ anything other than that. Paul's that way. He makes a point of going after what he wants and getting it. You're that way, too: You do whatever the hell you want and everybody has to deal with it.

I'm going to be that way, too. From now on.

Can't believe you disappeared. Where did you go? Are you still in New York? You could be dead for all I know. I went to your place. Landlady said she saw you one evening and the next afternoon your apartment was empty.

I ~~ain't got no business caring~~ shouldn't care. I do, though. But you and Paul have taught me to care about myself a lot more. I'm going to do that from now on, too.

Paul asked me to move in with him. I'm going to. He doesn't know that yet. I told him I'd think about it, but I had made up my mind to say yes before he asked me. I'll string him along for a while. He asks me every day—in person, in texts, on the phone. I tell him it's a big step, I'm not sure we're ready, there's a lot to consider. He's been asking—nagging—badgering—for a month. I'm playing it cool. Taking my time. Biding my time. When I say yes, it'll be on my own terms.

Sometimes I stop and think, *Damn. A famous artist wants me to move in with him. I must be OK.*

I'm on top of the world, Mel. I'm going to stay here, too.

Paul thinks he's in charge. He likes my submissiveness. What he thinks is my submissiveness. We ~~was at this party~~ were at a party a friend of his gave. I ~~got to talking~~ had a conversation with someone who said when it comes to older guys and younger guys, the older one always thinks he's in control, ~~'cause~~ since he ~~got~~ has the money. "But don't be fooled," he said, and leaned in close like he was sharing a dangerous and delicious secret. "It's the younger one who controls the relationship. Know why, Cedric? Because the older one will do whatever it takes to keep a young boyfriend on his arm, in his bed. It's not that young guys make older guys feel young again. It's that they make them feel relevant."

Paul likes telling me what to do in bed. Lie there. Flip over. Touch me here. Don't talk. It ~~ain't no big thing~~ isn't a big deal playing along. I like when he presses my face into his chest. The press is tender and hard at the same time, like he loves me, like I belong to him, like he'd rather kill than let me go. That's cool.

176

That's when I like him most.

We still fight. That's cool, too. It's who we are. We fight when he wants to be in control and I resist. He once made fun of me when I told him about you, Mel. I told him you and me I fought a lot because we saw the world differently. Paul laughed when I said that. But isn't that the same reason Paul and I fight? He wants control and I resist—isn't that the same as him trying to force his version of the world on me, and me fighting to keep the good parts of my own? His world is valid. So is mine. I know we can each have the best of both worlds. Paul hasn't figured that out yet. He's all black-and-white thinking, no oases of gray. Give and take: Another thing he hasn't figured out. He will.

Control is funny, though. It can shift. Subtly. Quietly. A crowning note in an aria that decrescendos to a murmur. Like the other night. I was on my side and he was in me, making love to me from behind, his chest against my back, and he was telling me not to move, to let him all the way in. "All the way, my dear," he said, and I whispered, "Paul. Paul. Kiss my scars. Kiss the scars on the back of my neck." And he did. And I wanted him to keep doing it, so I said, "Kiss them. There. And there. And there. And there. Good boy."

KISS THE SCARS: A PLAYLIST

Symphony No. 41 in C major (*Jupiter* Symphony)
Wolfgang Amadeus Mozart, completed 1788
Recommended recording: Josef Kripps & the
Concertgebouw Orchestra

Il Barbiere di Siviglia (The Barber of Seville)
Opera by Gioachino Rossini, premiered 1816
Recommended recording: Lawrence Brownlee, Nathan Gunn,
Elīna Garanča, Miguel Gómez-Martínez & the
Munich Radio Orchestra

L'elisir D'amore (The Elixer of Love)
Opera by Gaetano Donizetti, premiered 1832
Recommended recording: Kathleen Battle, Luciano Pavarotti,
Leo Nucci, Enzo Dara, Dawn Upshaw, James Levine
& The Metropolitan Opera Chorus and Orchestra

Tannhäuser
Opera by Richard Wagner, premiered 1845
Recommended recording: Grace Bumbry, Wolfgang
Windgassen, Victoria de los Ángeles, Wolfgang Sawallisch
& the Bayreuth Festival Orchestra and Chorus

Les Pêcheurs de Perles (The Pearl Fishers)
Opera by Georges Bizet, premiered 1863
Recommended recording: Barbara Hendricks, John Aler,
Gino Quilico, Michel Plasson,
Orchestra & Chorus of Capitole de Toulouse

La bohème
Opera by Giacomo Puccini, premiered 1896
Recommended recording: Barbara Hendricks, Jose Carreras,
Gino Quilico, James Conlon & the Orchestre
National de France

Tosca
Opera by Giacomo Puccini, premiered 1900
Recommended recording: Leontyne Price, Placido Domingo,
Sherill Milnes, Zubin Mehta & the Philharmonia Orchestra

Madama Butterfly
Opera by Giacomo Puccini, premiered 1904
Recommended recording: Leontyne Price, Richard Tucker,
Rosalind Elias, Erich Leinsdorf & the
RCA Italiana Orchestra and chorus

Ariadne auf Naxos
Opera by Richard Strauss, premiered 1912
Recommended recording: Jessye Norman, Edita Gruberova,
Julia Varady, Dietrich Fischer-Dieskau, Kurt Masur
& the Gewandhaus Orchestra and Chorus

"How Much Can I Stand," "Worried Blues,"
& "Wild Geese Blues"
Sung by Gladys Bentley, 1928

The Quintessential Billie Holiday Volumes 1–9
Recorded 1933 - 1942

The Complete Aladdin Recordings of Lester Young
Recorded 1942 - 1947

The Best of the Nat King Cole Trio
Recorded 1947-1950

"Salt Peanuts"
Dizzy Gillespie & Charlie Parker
From the album *The Quintet: Jazz at Massey Hall*, 1953

"Come Rain or Come Shine"
Sung by Dinah Washington
From the album *Dinah Jams*, 1955

"Make the Man Love Me"
Sung by Dinah Washington
From the album *For Those in Love*, 1955

"Pannonica"
Thelonious Monk
From the album *Brilliant Corners*, 1956

Kind of Blue
Album by Miles Davis, 1959

"The Surrey with the Fringe on Top"
Sung by Mel Tormé
From the album *Mel Tormé Swings Schubert Alley*, 1960

Ella Returns to Berlin
Album by Ella Fitzgerald, 1961

"The Masquerade Is Over"
Sung by Nancy Wilson
From the album *Nancy Wilson / Cannonball Adderly*, 1962

"Got to Be Real"
Sung by Cheryl Lynn
From the album *Cheryl Lynn*, 1978

"Don't Stop Till You Get Enough"
Sung by Michael Jackson
From the album *Off the Wall*, 1979

Colour by Numbers
Album by Culture Club, 1983

Debussy Mélodies
Album by Barbara Hendricks, 1985

"On My Own"
Sung by Patti LaBelle & Michael McDonald
From the album *Winner in You*, 1986

ACKNOWLEDGMENTS

Writing is a solitary (ad)venture, but you get a lot of help along the way. Each one of the stories in this collection was given nurturing feedback during the writing process. I want to express my appreciation to the people who made this collection possible: Nancy Agabian, Anthony Della Penna, Garth Greenwell, Scott Alexander Hess, Regina Jamison, Jonathan Jones, Alan Lessick, Nick Maglioti, Ann Podracky, Emily Raboteau, Russell Ricard, David Rompf, Jennifer Sabin, Jordan Schauer, Anna Voisard, Matt Waters, Justin P. Williams, and Sophie Ziner.

And a special shout-out to Brian Brennan who's always so dependable and insightful.

Thank you to Tim Fredrick, Jackie Sherbow, Heather Talty, Allison Escoto, Sokunthary Svay, and the entire *Newtown Literary* family for giving this loner a literary community to belong to.

Thank you to Michael Nava and Salem West, my editor and publisher respectively, for welcoming this collection to their publishing home.

And many, many, many thanks to my agent, Malaga Baldi, for not giving up on finding a home for this book even when I had.

ABOUT THE AUTHOR

Joe's debut novel *Jazz Moon*, set against the backdrop of the Harlem Renaissance and glittering Jazz Age Paris, was published by Kensington Books. It won the Publishing Triangle's prestigious Edmund White Award for Debut Fiction and was a finalist for a Lambda Literary Award. David Ebershoff, author of *The Danish Girl*, has called *Jazz Moon* "A passionate, alive, and original novel about love, race, and jazz in 1920s Harlem and Paris—a moving story of traveling far to find oneself."

His short stories have appeared *in Global City Review, The Piltdown Review, The New Engagement, Storychord, Penumbra, Promethean,* and *Shotgun Honey*. His work has been anthologized in *Love Stories from Africa, Best Gay Love Stories 2009, Best Gay Stories 2015,* and *Strength*. And his short story "Cleo" earned a Pushcart Prize nomination.

Joe served as Prose Editor for *Newtown Literary*, a journal dedicated to nurturing writers from Queens, New York, and he edited *Best Gay Stories 2017*.

Joe has led creative writing classes at Gotham Writers' Workshop, Newtown Literary/Queens Library, and the Bronx Council on the Arts. He has served on the planning committee for the Provincetown Book Festival.

Joe Okonkwo earned an MFA in Creative Writing from City College of New York. And he lives and writes in Queens, New York City.

Amble Press, an imprint of Bywater Books, publishes fiction and narrative nonfiction by LGBTQ writers, with a primary, though not exclusive, focus on LGBTQ writers of color. For more information on our titles, authors, and mission, please visit our website.

www.amblepressbooks.com

CPSIA information can be obtained
at www.ICGtesting.com
Printed in the USA
JSHW020007120821
17775JS00002B/2